YORK NOTES

General Editors: Professor A.N. Jeffares (*University of Stirling*) & Professor Suheil Bushrui (*American University of Beirut*)

Elechi Amadi

THE CONCUBINE

Notes by Roger Ebbatson
MA (SHEFFIELD) M PHIL (LONDON)
Senior Lecturer in English,
University of Sokoto, Nigeria

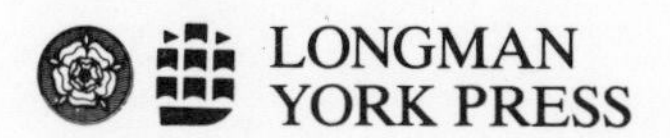
LONGMAN
YORK PRESS

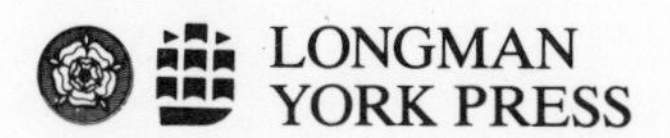

YORK PRESS
Immeuble Esseily, Place Riad Solh, Beirut.

LONGMAN GROUP LIMITED
Burnt Mill,
Harlow, Essex

First published 1981
ISBN 0 582 78248 1
Printed in Hong Kong by
Wilture Enterprises (International) Ltd.

Contents

Part 1
Introduction

The life of the author

Elechi Amadi was born in 1934 at Aluu near Port Harcourt in the south-east of Nigeria. He is a member of the Ikwerre minority ethnic group. He was educated at Government College, Umuahia, and graduated with a degree in mathematics and physics from University College, Ibadan. After working as a land-surveyor he entered the Nigerian Army in a teaching capacity and was posted to the Military School at Zaria where he gained the rank of captain. In 1965 he left the army to teach at the Anglican Grammar School, Igrito, near Port Harcourt. During the Nigerian Civil War (1967–70) Amadi was twice detained in the eastern sector. After his second release he joined the 3rd Marine Commandos in the Federal Army and was later appointed District Officer in Ahoada. Since the Civil War he has lived in Port Harcourt, working first as Acting Permanent Secretary in the Ministry of Information, then as Permanent Secretary in the Ministry of Education, Rivers State. Amadi is the author of three novels, a number of plays, and a book about his Civil War experiences.

A note on traditional Igbo life

The traditional villages of the Igbo people of eastern Nigeria were found in flat or gently undulating land away from the coast. To make sites for villages and for agriculture clearings were made in the forest, often close to a source of water. The vegetation consisted of dense undergrowth, and above this the trees of the great forest raised their heads—notably the *bombax* (silk cotton), *uroko* (African oak), and palm and coconut trees. The key geographical division was between the Igbo, who dwelt inland, and the Olu, a riverine people. The soil was fertile and great quantities of yams and catch-crops could be raised from it. In addition to yams the main crops were cassava, beans and maize. The farming year had clear-cut climatic divisions: the dry season ran from November to May, and began with a period of extremely dry winds from the north called the harmattan, a period when dust often obscured the sun; this was followed by the hot season until April, when tornadoes ushered in the rainy season, which extended until October.

The Igbo village was a community in which all adult males had a right to be heard. (A French visitor to the area commented that true liberty existed in Igboland, but its name was not inscribed on any monument.) Each village stood by itself in the forest or open grassland and there would be little interaction between one village and another; there might be friendly rivalry (as in *The Concubine*) or intermittent hostility—as in Amadi's second novel, *The Great Ponds* (1969). The Igbo tenaciously held on to a concept of village democracy in which every adult male could speak. But although each village may have stood as an isolated democratic unit, there were three ways of effecting wider relationships: firstly, through trade routes out to the south and the Niger delta (such operations were dominated by the Aro people, and included the sale of slaves); secondly, through marriage, since often the young men were obliged to marry outside their own village (as Ekwueme does), and thus kinship bonds were forged with surrounding communities; and thirdly, through a complex network of oracles placed throughout Igboland.

The land possessed by a family could not be taken away from them and all cases of land dispute (for instance, like that between Madume and Emenike at the beginning of the novel) would be settled by the village elders, whose word was law. Personal property, including wives and slaves, passed to the eldest surviving brother or other male relative. Wives generally had no rights over themselves or their own children. In such a patrilineal society great stress was placed upon producing a male heir (hence Madume's despair at his four daughters). Although palm-wine was the main drink, the village would use a local water supply for washing and other purposes. Huts would be placed at different angles to one another and there would be no symmetry in design. The terra-cotta walls were topped with thatch, and each house stood in its own compound surrounded by a thatched wall of varying height. The size of the compound depended more upon the space available than on the status of the owner; within the wall there would be a collection of huts of irregular shape and size, with floors of beaten clay. Inside, the huts would be littered with items such as wicker fish-traps, gourds used as palm-wine flagons, hoes, skins on the floor for seating (there would be no chairs), and a fire in the middle of the room. The beds were built on a simple frame over which a layer of offolaw (palm-stems) was fixed; occasionally the bed would be made of solid clay. The head of the household had his own hut, and each wife also had a hut which she shared with her own children. When the boys grew up they built themselves bachelor quarters inside their father's compound (as Ekwueme has done). Adjoining the head's private apartment was a recess containing the household gods.

Each compound possessed its own farm some distance off in the bush. By tilling the land a man could produce most of his food except for meat and fish, which would be a luxury bought outside the village (unless the man were a hunter, like Ekwueme). Each village had its own market, fetish-ground and meeting-place. The life of the men consisted of farming, hunting, wrestling and talking; that of the women centred upon the markets, cooking and preparation of food, and farming, by which they could raise some extra money for the children. The main foodstuff for all was pounded yam; the yam was boiled and then placed in a mortar and pounded with a pestle until it resembled dough. It would be eaten with soup cooked over the fire.

Marriage was the most significant event in life, and to be childless would be a disaster for a woman. In many cases the boy would choose his own bride, but frequently the parents selected a girl for him whilst he was still a child (as is the case with Ekwueme). Courtship in the Western sense was unknown; inquiries would be made about the girl's character, temper, marketing and cooking abilities; and then visits would begin to establish friendly relations between the two families. The boy himself would take little part in all this. After presentation of kegs of palm-wine and kola-nuts the negotiations could begin in earnest in order to fix the bride-price. This depended on the rank, age and personal qualities of the girl in question; once the first instalment was paid she was reckoned to be married. The girl was then received by the man's relatives and subjected to close scrutiny. The whole affair would be concluded by a great wedding-feast.

Neither boys nor girls knew their real age; they referred always to their 'otu', their age-group. The girls, before and after marriage, enjoyed decorating themselves with camwood dye or beautifully-executed patterns of 'uti' (indigo), adorning themselves with cowrie shells and beads, and making elaborate coiffures. In addition both sexes underwent cicatrisation—tattooing over the front part of the body.

The society was polygamous, but the first wife was accorded higher status than the others in the household and at public functions. The wife could not divorce the husband; if the man wished for a divorce, as Ekwueme does, it was a simple enough matter, and the girl's parents had to repay the bride-price and other expenses.

When a free-born man died the best possible arrangements had to be made. Suicides and other outcasts were regarded as having met their death through 'onwu ekwensu' (the agency of the devil), and their bodies were cast out into the 'bad bush' reserved for such cases. For ordinary deaths efforts were made to keep the spirit of the departed in contentment; a second burial was to ensure final acceptance of the departed in the spirit world to which he was supposed to have returned. God sent man into the world to fulfil certain functions and ensure that life continued on earth; after this the man could 'go home', but until the second burial was concluded the spirit of the dead man was inclined to haunt the village. After completion of these ceremonials the dead spirit remained in the world beyond until reincarnated again. The burials of big men, such as chiefs or kings, would be accompanied by ritual slaughter. The deaths of Emenike and Madume reflect these attitudes and rituals exactly.

The main social pastimes, as Amadi beautifully shows, were dancing and music, okwe (a game with counters), and wrestling (extensively dealt with in *The Great Ponds*). Education in the traditional Igbo village has been summarised by a historian of the period:

> The parents had their own way of bringing up their children to fit into life in the family compounds and the states. They imparted moral and religious education, with clear precepts reinforced by taboos. They gave training in the etiquette and conventions of society; they trained the minds of the children as they taught them to count yams and ears of corn, or to give answers to conundrums, or to repeat in their own words the fables of the family history. In the moonlight the children played games and told stories and learnt alliterative verses. As they grew older they were apprenticed to jobs or initiated into further mysteries of life.*

In the Igbo village community the physical aspect of nature was totally integrated into the experience of the people. There was no element of romantic nature-worship as in Western literature (as in, for instance, the poetry of Wordsworth). The Igbo lived consciously and subconsciously within nature itself. Their folklore and myth drew symbolism from nature. In particular, the forest became a prime source of power both natural and supernatural, both a real place and a mystery. The mystery was understood, and to some extent controlled, by ritual formulations of the priests. The chief deities were a supreme being, Chukwu, and a devil, Ekwensu. Certain acts, such as murder, theft, and adultery, would be offences against the will of the gods. There were many and varied sacred objects in Igbo traditional religion: cows, sheep, monkeys, fish, snakes (held to be immortal because they shed their skin—the python was especially venerated), tortoises, rocks, trees and streams. These objects were not worshipped in themselves but as habitations of the spirits; in addition each household had its own gods. Worship was not directed to the supreme deity, but to two other objects of worship: the ancestors (Ndiche) and the forces of nature. Magical power was believed to reside in charms, medicines and ritual acts. The world was thus conceived by the Igbo people as an arena which witnessed the interplay of psychic and physical forces. Shrines were found in most villages to the gods of thunder and lightning (whose symbol was a tree with two pots in front of it), and the earth-goddess (Ala, Ale or Ane),

*J.F.A. Ajayi: *Christian Missions in Nigeria*, Longman, London, 1965, p.133.

who was connected with the cult of the ancestors and dominated public morals.

The moral scale of values was validated by the religious values of the society; religion naturally entailed clear social obligations and duties. Sacrifices were constantly needed as part of this system (as we see in the case of Madume's injury, or in the efforts to bind the Sea-King); unless sacrifice was made the lives and interests of the people would be harmed. The gods' demands were indicated by their executive on earth, the dibia (seer). The dibia, such a key figure in *The Concubine*, had a dual function: to explain supernatural events and make misfortune intelligible, and to prescribe the necessary sacrifices. This was a society ruled by gods and ancestors, in which the religious and everyday were intermingled. In particular the Igbo way of life stressed the idea of recurrence: the lunar month, the seasons and the farming year, and the reincarnation of the ancestors (Ndiche—'the returners'). God had created the visible universe, 'uwa', and the spirit world, 'alusi'. The spirits would punish those, like Emenike, Madume and Ekwueme, who unwittingly infringed upon their rights. Thus the dibia exerted a key role in dealing with the spirits and held an exalted place in the community. Sacrifice was made to appease unfamiliar spirits who are shrouded in mystery but can be located as authors of the present trouble. It was common practice to place the blame for village troubles upon a woman who would be accused of witchcraft—we see a variant of this in the treatment of Ihuoma as a fatal woman.

Another feature of the Igbo religious code was that of the personal spirit, the 'chi'. This might be identified as the 'guardian angel', and it was seen as a man's other identity in the spirit world, complementary to that he enjoyed in the human world. This idea had its origins in Igbo duality: the man had a 'double' in the spirit world. The 'chi' had unprecedented power over a man's destiny, and a bad 'chi' could harm a man's fortunes. The term derives from 'Chi Ukwu', the name for the Great Chi or supreme being, and in Igbo cosmology there was a complex relationship between Chukwu, the sun, and the 'chi'. Although Amadi fails to make the distinction clear, the 'chi' should be differentiated from the activities of the 'agwu' which plagues Ahurole in *The Concubine*. This would be a minor spirit normally attendant upon seers or people with special gifts. In Ahurole's case it makes her awkward and peevish. The tolerance extended to her would not apply to persons who were genuinely rebelling against the communal order, as the portrait of Tuere in *The Voice* (1964) by Gabriel Okara (*b*.1921) shows us. Amadi glances at the operations of the 'chi' when he says, of Emenike's defeat, that 'a man's god may be away on a journey on the day of an important fight' (p.5).

The Concubine is dominated by the unseen presence of the Sea-King.

Many tribes of south-east Nigeria regarded water superstitiously, and attributed magical powers to spirits inhabiting both sea and fresh water. Such spirits were generally felt to be hostile and alien to mankind, and reflected the communal fear of water (few members of such tribes could swim). The activities of water-spirits should be contrasted with the kindly disposition of earth-spirits—the earth being seen as mother and provider of sustenance. Possession by water-spirits was a common belief, and it was usually women who were allegedly so possessed: in a male dominated society women were thought of as an unstable, shifting element—hence the irony of Ihuoma, the most stable and mature of women, being associated with the malevolent power of the Sea-King.

In addition to religious sanctions the life of the village was dominated by strict etiquette, as exemplified by the taking of kola-nut at the opening of discussions, or the need to salute one's neighbour on every occasion one encountered him. This element of repetition was stressed by the value placed on proverbs, fables and folk-lore. Igbo society was one in which residual folk memory was of the most crucial importance. Proverbs briefly express wisdom gained over many centuries of communal living. By uttering proverbial sayings the individual speaker acknowledged the supreme authority of the society at large; proverbs 'communalised' the speaker. Although Amadi uses proverbial phrases in a more restrained manner than Chinua Achebe (*b.*1930) this feature of *The Concubine* also helps to show how firmly the life of the people is based in ancient memory. Materials were transmitted by oral tradition either by word of mouth or by custom and practice. The traditional tales often expressed man's cautious approach to life beyond the immediate family circle, and confidence in his own kinship group. The oral tradition originated in and reflected Igbo republicanism; thus Igbo culture could be contrasted with that of Europe which was aristocratic in origin, owing its foundation to systems of feudal patronage. A speaker who could use language effectively and had a good command of idioms in the Igbo village was widely respected and likely to become a leader of the community. In Igbo traditional society there was an intricate interdependence between patterns of livelihood, social relations, and dogmatic belief about the nature of the world and man's place within it. The central family unit stressed unity, solidarity and a sense of common destiny: as the Igbo saying went, 'When the eye weeps, the nose weeps with it'. The aim of oral tradition was to inculcate in the young a sense of right and wrong behaviour and social duty. To this end folk tales endowing animals with human qualities were invented, the usual figures being the tortoise, spider, hare, rabbit or praying mantis. The stress of such tales fell upon parental responsibility, respect for the elders, grace in women, virility and heroism in men, and social justice. An illustration of this is the tale of the chicken who had no time to attend a meeting of all the animals but agreed to abide by any decisions reached. This particular meeting was convened to decide which animal should be offered to man for use as a sacrifice, and of course the chicken was unanimously elected: the moral being that everyone must play his part in the life of the community. The stories constantly stressed the precedence of group over individual loyalties; some social norms were so sacred that anyone who broke them would be branded as an outcast.

The strength of such living Igbo traditions can scarcely be overestimated in reading African fiction. The music, art and story-telling traditions of a whole way of life lie behind *The Concubine*. The idyllic atmosphere owes much to the spontaneity and ease of rhythm expressed in song and dance, and the dance especially is the perfect embodiment of that group participation so characteristic of Igbo village life. Even deeper lies the influence of oral literature, which has justly been described as the springboard of all written literature in such societies. From these sources in the culture of Africa Amadi has moulded the vision of life which he presents in *The Concubine*.

The world of Amadi's novels

The leading Nigerian novelist Chinua Achebe formulated some years ago what he felt to be the starting-point in the writing of fiction by Africans, and the theme which the African novelist should be concerned to project to his audience:

> This theme, put quite simply, is that the African peoples did not hear of culture for the first time from Europeans; that their societies were not mindless but frequently had a philosophy of great depth and value and beauty, that they had poetry and, above all, they had dignity. It is this dignity that many African peoples all but lost in the colonial period, and it is this that they must now regain.*

Amadi's novels might have been written in strict accordance with this precept. He writes of village life in pre-colonial eastern Nigeria; his concern is with a society which was stable, unlike that portrayed in Achebe's classic *Things Fall Apart*, where a similar society is shown in collision with the new colonial masters. Achebe's stress upon the value of old and known ways of life is especially relevant when studying Amadi; the concerns of his novels were well expressed earlier by the Irish poet W.B. Yeats (1865–1939):

> How but in custom and in ceremony
> Are innocence and beauty born?

As with other so-called 'regional novelists' (that is, writers who devote

*'The role of the writer in a new nation', *Nigeria Magazine*, 81 (June 1964), p.157.

themselves to writing about a small closely-observed area) there is great emphasis in Amadi upon the village as the 'good place'—the centre and register of the values of the characters, even those who try to rebel against such values. Amadi insists upon the local as the source of all that is truly known and experienced by his people: the Igbo village is a close-knit community in a sense which could never be true of a modern city. The world as seen by Amadi thus contrasts markedly with the modern urbanised Africa of a writer like Cyprian Ekwensi. Amadi gives to the reader a lovingly accurate picture of village life undisturbed by intrusive forces of colonialism, nationalism or industrialism. In this society all members are interdependent, bound together by religious, social and economic ties. Little is known of more distant places or alien cultures: Amadi's characters must seek their happiness and livelihood within the local community. This is a stable rather than a stagnant society. Each Amadi novel has a sense of movement and development that drives the characters; they are in the grip of communal forces greater than themselves.

Amadi does not, however, present a wholly idyllic picture. He is careful not to suggest that the pastoral Igbo led a continuously happy round of wrestling contests, harvesting feasts, courtship, marriage celebrations and the like. On the contrary, each of his novels has a tragic outcome which also derives from the essential nature of the society. Indeed the overriding themes in Amadi are first, the clash between human and divine will, and second, the coercive power of communal opinion. The divine will is most often felt in the form of a natural force; the gods who matter here are gods of thunder, earth, sea, night and so on. During his imprisonment in the Civil War Amadi once reflected that 'life was a bitter, cruel dream, arranged by a sadistic god'. This was written at a time of mental and physical suffering and leaves out of account the joy, beauty and instinctive wisdom of traditional life as portrayed in the novels; but it has some truth as a statement of Amadi's view of the relationship between man and his gods in this remote world. Within this perspective a man's relationships with his fellow-men and women, though important, are governed by his religious attitudes and relation with the supernatural. It is in clashes between freedom of individual will and the unyielding gods that tragedy arises.

In his choice of theme we can locate much of Amadi's interest as a writer: although he limits himself to a narrow traditional society and to a set of ostensibly simple unsophisticated people, he actually takes as his theme one of the most crucial of all for mankind—his relation with nature. Amadi's novels are not, therefore, simply love stories in a homely village setting; they have universal applications for the reader. Each of the novels turns upon the struggles of the individual within the community, struggles which are seen in a fatalistic light. Amadi is very adept at picturing not only living individuals such as Ihuoma and Ekwueme in *The Concubine*, Olumba in *The Great Ponds*, or Olumati in *The Slave* (1978), but also in showing the community itself as a living organism to which all are vitally connected, for better or worse. An organism is a body in which all the parts are vitally interrelated; thus matters of love, sex, marriage, property, and religion can never be decided by the individual alone. All decisions, wishes and actions need to be supported and accepted by the community at large. The individual is thus supported by the social organism; but he may also become the victim of coercive social and religious orthodoxy. In handling this subject Amadi shows great delicacy and tact. He is aware of the strength and sanity of the life of his ancestors, but also demonstrates how the communal life can bring about general tragedy. One of his key concerns is to show how opinion and belief can shape and determine the course of an individual life, and it may be hinted that the force of this belief is actually more potent than the supposed intervention of the gods into the scheme of things. At first all the tragedy of *The Concubine* seems to flow from the opening scene, when Emenike is injured. Gradually, as the tragedy accumulates, this explanation is replaced: we are witnessing the interference of the gods, with increasingly dreadful results. We are seeing subtly how the *belief* in supernatural domination works to destroy human happiness. Amadi sees life in a way that might be called 'deterministic': it has been ordained by the gods that Ihuoma should exert a fatal attraction upon man, and if such gods do not exist in 'reality' they do so most powerfully in the minds of the villagers of Omokachi. It is this pervasive belief that determines the reaction to the plight of Ihuoma, Olumba or Olumati. The plight of Ihuoma provides the tragic thrust of *The Concubine*.

Tragedy is an ancient literary form in which things end badly. If *The Concubine* does not meet the formal definition of tragedy as the fall of a great man, it does (like other tragic works) show us people broken by forces they cannot overcome or comprehend. The damage inflicted by tragedy is irreparable: there could be no question of compensation for the degree of suffering involved. Tragic literature shows us the limitations of reason and justice by demonstrating how the gods or fates mock and destroy man at will. In some tragic texts the terror of the events leads to new insight and repose; but in other works, as in *The Concubine*, the action ends bleakly with no suggestion of mercy. The dignity of man in tragedy lies in his stoical, uncomplaining acceptance of suffering; in this sense the people of Omokachi are advanced tragedians.

The careful student will appreciate that this is not the whole story. The life of the village, shot through with a sense of fatality though it may be, is also marked by vivacity, movement, joy, and communal brotherhood. Amadi's people enjoy a close working relationship with the seasons, the earth and the plants and animals, and celebrations of that relationship in feasting, song and dance are high points of the novel. The villagers do not feel alienated from their own society in the way of many characters in modern fiction; they experience a relationship with the earth like that of a baby to its mother. There are many memorable scenes expressing this closeness and joy, and when reading we should balance these against the overall tragedy. Whilst the progression of the tale is marked by a series of ghastly experiences which befall the various characters, the tone—right up to the last page—is lightened by Amadi's descriptions of traditional pastimes and pleasures. Yet at the end the full weight of human tragedy and helplessness are felt: a young and personable couple are finally brought together after periods of unhappiness and uncertainty and look forward to settling down together, when a stray arrow kills the young man.

The Concubine sets the pattern of a close-knit communal life, celebrating existence, love and a working intimacy with nature, which is darkened by forces beyond the power of man to understand or control. In *The Great Ponds* Amadi delineates the disintegration not just of individual happiness, but of a total community; in the second novel a sense of gloom pervades the whole action, which concerns inter-village rivalry over possession of some forest lakes. Only in the final paragraph does Amadi briefly indicate that all the disasters ascribed by the villagers to the vengeance of the gods in fact have a medical explanation. The third novel, *The Slave*, deals with the problem of a family cursed with the shadow of slavery and of a young man's efforts to shake off this curse. Each of the novels endorses the advice of the powerful hero of *The Great Ponds* to his friend: 'Never play with the gods, my son. They are powerful and should be respected. I would rather face a whole village in battle than have the weakest of the gods after me.'

Many students of *The Concubine* ask why the people involved should believe such crude superstitions. The question is a natural one, but reveals a misunderstanding of how the society is conceived and dramatised in the novel. The ritual practised by the old Igbo peoples is characteristic of isolated groups. The 'code' of their religious belief, and the language they use to refer to it, is restricted and limited; it can only have real meaning where all members of the society know one another. The rites they practise give them group solidarity, and their religious ideas often carry punitive overtones. Their cosmology (their view of the universe) is part of the intricate social bond which, it is implied, has been formed over long periods of years. The system of strict social control exercised in such a traditional society has to be acceptable to its members by appealing to ultimate beliefs about the nature of man and his world. Where such pressure is strong, as in the Igbo villages, there is no room for individualism or the development of private ideas. The villagers can think only what the system of beliefs evolved by their ancestors *allows* them to think. The shared experience of the entire community influences the consciousness of the individual. Social pressure is too great to allow much freedom of will; these effects are examined here in Ekwueme's struggle to renege on his betrothal to Ahurole, and on an extended scale in Gabriel Okara's *The Voice*. The society Amadi presents to the reader is characterised by a public system of rights and duties which gives to each person his full identity—the characters here know from an early age what to eat, how to address one another, how to dress, how to get married, how to bury someone, and so on. Even the priests fall under this pressure; the only outsiders would be foreigners, of whom there are none, or those committing abominations (for instance, Madume, who commits suicide, or Olumati in *The Slave*). Co-ordination of the whole village is demonstrated by piety towards authority, and therefore, as Amadi sympathetically explains in *The Slave*, there comes into being a category of rejects. The Igbo cosmology has to deal with demonic powers and the actions of the spirits, and justice in the human sense is not necessarily a feature of that plan. The emphasis falls upon the honour of the individual in a universe divided between warring forces of good and evil.

This is the universe of Elechi Amadi as the student of *The Concubine* should try to understand it. Such understanding may be furthered by referring to a passage in *Sunset in Biafra* (1973) where Amadi contemplates the landscapes of the Zaria region of Northern Nigeria:

> Against the background of the hills and wide plains, the frailty and the insignificance of man are revealed in stunning perspective. Man's cares and passions become ridiculous, his most purposeful activities a mere dance in the silence of space—a mad, futile, purposeless dance without spectators. At night, against the dome of stars, the earth becomes a ball of dirt, and man the pitiful fungus growing on it.

Yet if man may sometimes appear to be a 'pitiful fungus', he is also blessed with energy, beauty, joy and moral values. Amadi gives Africa an image of itself: a communal life which, for all its tensions, fatalism and tragedy, the reader feels to have possessed beauty, dignity and deep human values, values deriving from a specific set of long-held traditions. The student needs to grasp the significance of such values and traditions before he can profitably study the text in detail.

A note on the text

The Concubine was first published by Heinemann Educational Books, London, in the African Writers Series, 25, 1966; it was reset and reprinted in 1977. All page references in these Notes are to the 1977 edition.

Part 2

Summaries

of THE CONCUBINE

A general summary

The novel concerns the life and loves of Ihuoma, a beautiful and widely-admired young woman living in a small traditional village community in the east of Nigeria. Her first husband, Emenike, a popular and vigorous young man, is injured in a fight with his rival, Madume, and subsequently dies of 'lock-chest'. Some time later Madume, who is a blustering bully, presses unwelcome attentions upon Ihuoma. While illegally harvesting from her land he is blinded by a spitting cobra and, depressed by his situation, commits suicide. The widowed Ihuoma is admired by Ekwueme, a young man of the village. Ekwueme, however, has been betrothed to another girl since childhood, and he reluctantly agrees to marry her. Ekwueme is a likeable character, but has been badly spoilt by his mother. He makes a mess of his marriage to the childish Ahurole who, in order to assure herself of his love, secretly administers a love-potion to Ekwueme. The results of the potion prove disastrous: Ekwueme falls ill, behaves strangely, runs away from the village, and eventually divorces Ahurole.

Ihuoma plays a key part in bringing about Ekwueme's cure and return to normality, and his love for her grows stronger. Marriage negotiations are finally begun between the two parties, but at this point the village seer reveals the truth about Ihuoma: she is the wife of the powerful and jealous Sea-King. Contrary to the Sea-King's wishes she has sought incarnation as a human being. Although the god is angry at this, she is his favourite wife and he allows her a normal life-span on earth; but he wreaks vengeance on any mortal who seeks her love in marriage. Ihuoma's only permitted role, it appears, would be that of a man's female companion or concubine. Ekwueme determines to press on with the marriage plans, and is arranging the ingredients for a sacrifice to control the activities of the Sea-King when he is accidentally killed by an arrow shot by Ihuoma's young son: the god has struck for a third time.

A note on the names

Names often have special significance in Igbo, and an appreciation of this adds to our understanding of the novel.

Emenike: a child given by the gods
Madume: relations are better than wealth
Ekwueme: member of a steadfast family
Wigwe: one who comes from the heavens
Adaku: a girl who will bring good fortune to the family
Ahurole: 'how many have you seen?'
Nnenda: my mother's mother
Wodu Wakiri: an individual worth more than ten people combined
Wonuma: good luck
Wagbara: a man without title
Nwonna: beauty associated with the shining of a gold bangle
Agwoturumbe: the snake that stings a tortoise (i.e. someone who is clever)
Ihuoma: bringer of good luck
Anyika: fortune-teller

Detailed summaries

Chapter 1

Emenike, a young man on his way to tap palm wine in the forest, is intercepted by his fellow-villager, Madume. He and Madume have just quarrelled over the ownership of a piece of land which has been awarded to Emenike. Madume, a jealous, quick-tempered and powerfully-built man, challenges his rival to fight. After a struggle Madume throws Emenike painfully against a jagged tree-stump and flees. Emenike staggers home and is met by his beautiful young wife, Ihuoma. The whole village learns of the fight, and Madume is relieved to hear that Emenike is still alive.

NOTES AND GLOSSARY:

iroko trunk: a thick trunk of a tree like an oak frequently a sacred tree in Africa hence Madume is strongly-built
calabash: bowl made from a dried gourd
whitlows: inflammatory tumours around the fingernail
rites of purification: sacrifice made to appease the spirit of a dead man and purify the land on which he was killed

Chapter 2

A sketch of Madume's character: although now in his thirties, he is unsuccessful and has produced only daughters. He is jealous and grasping, and especially envious of the handsome and popular Emenike for marrying Ihuoma. Emenike's brother, Nnadi, worried by his injuries, sends for Anyika, the mysterious dibia (seer and herbalist). In an atmosphere of gloom Anyika performs ritual divinations. Ihuoma nurses her husband devotedly. The following morning he is visited by friends, including Wodu Wakiri, the village jester, and Nwokekoro, the respected rainmaker.

NOTES AND GLOSSARY:

village age-group: a group of one's contemporaries, three years being usually bracketed together

plantain trees: tropical herbaceous tree with fruit resembling the banana

manillas: metal bracelet used as medium of exchange

libation: drink offered to the gods

divination cowries: shell of small gastropod used as currency in West Africa

divinations: the utilising of magical procedures to foretell the future

wrapper: cloth worn as a dress by the women

Chapter 3

Emenike gradually recovers and the family enjoys a meal of maize cobs. Now that her husband feels better Ihuoma is able to attend to her personal appearance again, and she begins to examine her hair-style. She is gentle, reserved and mature, and often mediates in the quarrels of the older women. Hearing an oduma dance in nearby Omigwe village she dances to herself, not realising that her husband is watching her performance admiringly.

NOTES AND GLOSSARY:

Eke: a market day. There were four days in the traditional Igbo calendar, arranged into eight per week: Nkwo, Eke, Orie, Afo; there were seven native weeks to a month

embraced her in the traditional way: that is, without kissing

Chapter 4

A description of the general topography: Omokachi, the scene of the story, is a small village of eleven family groups; distant in the east lies Aliji, and closer at hand in the west is Chiolu; the nearest village is Omigwe, which was founded by a man from Omokachi. The chief deities are Amadioha, the god of thunder, and Ojukwu, the bringer of smallpox, whose sacred bird is the vulture. Emenike accompanies the elders to the shrine of Amadioha to give thanks for his recovery. The atmosphere is threatening. Gazing at the priest's face as he performs the ceremonial rites, Emenike feels a premonition of death, and stares in fascination at the sacred snake as it devours the wing of a sacrificial chicken.

NOTES AND GLOSSARY:

one of his babies cut its upper teeth first: the cutting of the first tooth was keenly awaited by the Igbo community. If the lower tooth came first there was general rejoicing; the appearance of the first tooth in the upper jaw resulted in the child being thrown out into the 'bad bush'

yams: edible tuber of a type of tropical climbing plant

alligator pepper: a fruit containing small peppery seeds, used in sprinkling over kola-nut

orepe brand: a type of tree

Chapter 5

A few days later Emenike is dead of 'lock-chest' and Ihuoma gazes wistfully at his grave in the compound. She cannot believe that he is dead, but her reverie is interrupted by Wolu, Madume's wife. Suppressing a desire to blame Madume for Emenike's death, Ihuoma breaks down and cries. As Wolu leaves, Ihuoma's mother, Okachi, comes in and advises her daughter to be more stoical—advice which is seconded by Ekwueme, a young man of the village. The conversation turns to inter-village rivalry and wrestling contests, and Ihuoma feels a little more cheerful.

NOTES AND GLOSSARY:

'lock-chest': bronchitis

Chapter 6

Ekwueme, leaving Ihuoma's compound, reflects longingly upon the young widow's attractions. He meets his friend Wodu Wakiri, the village jester, and the two compose a song in honour of the dead Emenike. A month after Emenike's death an oduma dance is held and the song is performed. Ihuoma listens from her bed. She is in mourning and feels that life can never be the same again. In a dream Emenike returns and asks to be fed. On awaking, Ihuoma weeps sadly.

NOTES AND GLOSSARY:

foo-foo: pounded yam

Chapter 7

A year after Emenike's death the second burial rites are held. Ihuoma, aided by her brother-in-law Nnadi and his wife, makes all the necessary preparations. Old women arrive for the feast; then the young men indulge in a frenzied ritual dance and mock wrestling-match. Once the rites are successfully accomplished Ihuoma can put off her widow's weeds. She allows her friend Nnenda to plait her hair and decorate her body with indigo patterns, but reflects that beauty seems to be associated with sadness.

Chapter 8

Ihuoma and her three children visit her parents at Omigwe. As they prepare the food for a meal Okachi, Ihuoma's mother, advises her daughter to encourage Ekwueme's approaches. After a lighthearted family meal Okachi repeats her advice, but Ihuoma angrily rejects it and hurries home upset and confused.

Chapter 9

The rainy season is approaching, and Nnadi arranges for Ihuoma's roof to be re-thatched. He is helped by Wodu and Ekwueme, and when the work is done they all enjoy Ihuoma's cooking. The party breaks up but Ekwueme lingers behind. He tries to tell Ihuoma of his feelings for her, but is abashed by her air of mature detachment and retreats to his own compound where he irritably refuses the food prepared by his mother and sister. He has a threatening dream involving Emenike, and obtains protective charms from the dibia. Later Ekwueme hunts and finally kills an antelope in the forest.

Chapter 10

Madume reflects upon Emenike's death, for which he feels partly guilty. He concludes that the young man's death was the will of the gods, however, and determines to claim the disputed land from Ihuoma. Furthermore, he will now seize this second opportunity to make Ihuoma his wife. When he confides in Wolu, his wife, she is upset and refuses to approach Ihuoma on his behalf. Madume goes to Ihuoma's compound to speak to her, but injures his foot and returns home humiliated and annoyed. The injury necessitates a consultation with Anyika; the dibia explains that a number of spirits, including Emenike's father, are seeking vengeance on Madume. Elaborate sacrifices will be needed to appease them.

NOTES AND GLOSSARY:

Chineke: the supreme deity, 'god who creates'

Chapter 11

Nnenda, Ihuoma's neighbour, visits Ekwueme's household and talks to his parents, Wigwe and Adaku. Ekwueme accompanies her home and asks her to tell Ihuoma he admires her greatly. On a walk to the farms Nnenda relays the message but Ihuoma makes no response. Ekwueme waits anxiously for a reply.

NOTES AND GLOSSARY:

egbe-ohia: a large boil caused by a weed growing in the bush

Chapter 12

Having performed the prescribed sacrifices, Madume decides that it will now be safe for him to harvest plantains from the piece of land in dispute. Finding Ihuoma already at the site he quarrels with her and handles her roughly. She reports his misbehaviour and the villagers seek to restrain him. Madume reacts by going to cut down a bunch of plantains, but in doing so disturbs a cobra which spits venom into his eyes. Despite the ministrations of Wolu, his wife, and the dibia, Madume goes blind. He becomes an embittered man and the elders try unsuccessfully to persuade him to treat Wolu more considerately. She finally takes refuge with her parents. Next morning Madume is found hanged; as he committed suicide, his body must be carried to that part of the forest reserved for the disposal of outcasts.

NOTES AND GLOSSARY:

opolipo leaves: herbal leaf used medicinally

Abah: an exclamation of sorrow

Chapter 13

Nnenda and Ihuoma chat, but are interrupted by the arrival of Wakiri and Ekwueme. They make arrangements to tie up Ihuoma's yams the following day. Left alone with Ihuoma, Ekwueme once more feels tongue-tied and incapable of revealing his true feelings. Returning home he repairs his mother's kitchen-wall and later takes part in a dance rehearsal.

NOTES AND GLOSSARY:

Ofo and Ogu: gods who will defend an innocent person and avenge his wrongs

Chapter 14

Next day Wodu Wakiri, Ekwueme and Nnadi co-operate in tying up Ihuoma's yams at her farm. Ekwueme shares the evening meal with Ihuoma and tells her he wishes to marry her. But Ihuoma now reminds him that he has been betrothed to Ahurole since childhood, and declares that she herself intends to remain a widow, devoted to Emenike's memory. Ekwueme's parents, suspicious of the developing situation, determine to open marriage negotiations for Ahurole as soon as possible.

NOTES AND GLOSSARY:

'one can't eat a crab in secret': because of the noise

Chapter 15

At Omigwe, Ahurole and her friend Titi chatter about marriage. Ahurole is beautiful but moody, and she feels uncertain about her attitude to the forthcoming visit of Ekwueme's family and the ensuing marriage negotiations. She is quarrelsome and easily upset, and this is attributed to the influence of her personal spirit.

Chapter 16

Interviewed by Adaku, his mother, Ekwueme asserts that he has no wish to marry Ahurole, and finally admits that he loves Ihuoma. Fearing public censure, Wigwe, his father, informs Ekwueme that negotiations for Ahurole will start the following day. Ekwueme pleads his love for Ihuoma, and Wigwe reluctantly agrees to postpone matters whilst Ihuoma is consulted. Ekwueme races off to find her, but is unsuccessful.

Chapter 17

Nnenda tells Ihuoma that Ekwueme has been searching for her. While she is puzzling over this, Wigwe and Ekwueme arrive for an unorthodox evening visit. Although he is going against convention, Wigwe asks for Ihuoma's hand on behalf of his son. As has been anticipated, Ihuoma is compelled by etiquette to refuse this offer, and Ekwueme is humiliated in front of his father. The next day he disappears, but returns in the evening having killed a deer in the forest. Ihuoma feels insulted by the visit, and when Ekwueme sends her a present of venison via her son she turns angrily on the child.

Chapter 18

The interview has placed Ekwueme in an impossible position, and he unhappily accompanies the party who are to open negotiations for Ahurole. The talks begin with the appointment of an intermediary who will act on Wigwe's behalf. Ahurole avoids Ekwueme on his visits to her father's compound, and the young man finds her behaviour puzzling. Ahurole makes the traditional return visit to Wigwe's house at Omokachi, and Ihuoma calls to congratulate the girl on her marriage.

NOTES AND GLOSSARY:

ojongo hair style: a type of plaiting with hair gathered at the top of the head

Chapter 19

Ihuoma feels a sense of relief that Ekwueme is to marry Ahurole. She has a strong liking for Ekwueme but suppresses it in order to preserve the traditional properties and customs of the village. She now feels able to converse in a relaxed manner with Ekwueme when she meets him at a dance.

Chapter 20

Six months after the start of negotiations, Ahurole is officially installed as Ekwueme's wife. Ekwueme feels it is now incumbent upon him to behave in a more adult fashion, but in truth he is still devoted to his mother and continues to enjoy her food. A sketch of his boyhood shows how, as an only child for nearly twelve years, Ekwueme had been spoilt and was consequently despised by the other boys. Later his prowess at fighting and hunting restored his prestige, but he continues to compare all other women unfavourably with his mother. After their first meal alone together Ahurole and Ekwueme quarrel and Adaku has to intervene.

Chapter 21

Ekwueme recognises the problems he faces in his relationship with the moody Ahurole, but gradually becomes indifferent to his young wife. His father advises forbearance but Ekwueme can only dream longingly of Ihuoma. After another quarrel Ekwueme beats Ahurole who takes refuge with her parents at Omigwe. The case is brought to arbitration by the elders and the couple are reconciled, but they begin to avoid one another and the gap between them widens.

Chapter 22

Strolling home from a waterside market one evening the depressed Ekwueme converses with Ihuoma, but she is embarrassed when he starts to complain of Ahurole and is relieved to reach Omokachi. A few days later, as Ihuoma is harvesting her cocoyams, she is joined by Ekwueme, who feels happier when talking to her. But when he reappears the following day Ihuoma reprimands him for wilfully ignoring public opinion. She confides in Nnenda, who sympathises with the problems of the beautiful young widow.

NOTES AND GLOSSARY:

the Rikwos: a riverine people

Chapter 23

Ahurole's prized goat goes missing and Ekwueme goes round the village in search of the animal. He makes inquiries of Ihuoma, but the suspicious Ahurole, seeing him leaving the widow's compound, berates him for his unfaithfulness. He goes to Wodu for advice and the two men try to forget their miseries in song. Ahurole goes to Omigwe to discuss her marital troubles with her mother, and the old woman advises her daughter to administer a love-potion to Ekwueme to gain his permanent affection. When Ahurole requests Anyika to supply such a potion the dibia refuses, fearful of the effects it might have on Ekwueme's character. On learning of this, Wonuma, Ahurole's mother, declares that she will travel to Chiolu to see a second dibia.

Chapter 24

Wonuma goes to Chiolu and obtains the potion. The following evening Ahurole gives her husband soup containing the drug and within days Ekwueme suffers a succession of illnesses which leave him listless and indifferent to life. Ekwueme's parents begin to suspect that he has been bewitched, and when Wigwe talks to his son Ekwueme laughs rudely in his face and later runs away.

NOTES AND GLOSSARY:

ogbara: a stinging type of climbing plant

Chapter 25

Wigwe tries to intercept his son's flight out of the compound, but is knocked to the ground. Now thoroughly alarmed he gathers a small party and goes in search of Ekwueme. Ahurole, returning from the farm along a forest path, is surprised to see her husband running wildly towards her. Noticing him foaming at the mouth she hides in the bush, but he chases her. Men from the village intervene and escort Ekwueme home, but he escapes from custody and disappears. Wigwe and Adaku, consulting Anyika, now learn the truth about Ahurole and the love-potion. A search party is sent into the dark forest, and the elders pass the night in talk. Ekwueme's parents are frightened that the potion has driven him mad.

Chapter 26

When day dawns the search party returns empty-handed. The villagers gather for discussions, and learn that Ahurole has fled in disgrace. After further exploration Ekwueme is located sitting up a tree near the village armed with a club. Despite the entreaties of his parents and friends he refuses to come down, and the villagers conclude that he has gone mad. He demands to see Ihuoma, and when she appears he climbs quietly down the tree.

Chapter 27

Anyika seeks to cure Ekwueme, who is rude, vacant and inattentive. The young man refuses to accept medicine until Ihuoma agrees to marry him. Wigwe pleads with Ihuoma and she agrees to visit Ekwueme. In her presence he improves, takes his medicine and performs his ablutions. Returning later in the day Ihuoma finds Ekwueme's senses completely restored, and feels shy and uncomfortable at being closeted alone with him.

Chapter 28

Ekwueme makes a speedy recovery and begins trapping again. He spends all his spare time with Ihuoma, who now gracefully accepts his attentions. Eventually Ekwueme proposes to marry Ihuoma and divorces Ahurole. Everyone is gratified, with one exception—Anyika, the dibia. Performing a divination for Ekwueme's parents, he reveals that Ihuoma is a goddess, most valued of the Sea-King's wives. Incarnated in human form against his wishes, she is destined to bring disaster to all her lovers. Her only permitted human role is that of concubine. Ekwueme, on being informed that she has already caused the deaths of Madume and Emenike, expresses his intention to have his own way and marry Ihuoma. She herself is to be kept in the dark about the divination. Ekwueme therefore mentions nothing of this to Ihuoma; instead he tells her that the marriage negotiations will go ahead as planned.

Chapter 29

Ekwueme's parents decide that a second, more distinguished, dibia should be seen. With this in view Wigwe and Ekwueme journey to Aliji to consult the famous Agwoturumbe. Although he initially confirms Anyika's assessment of the situation, Agwoturumbe delights his visitors by asserting that he can bind the powers of the Sea-King and enable the marriage to go ahead. He explains that sacrifices must be made from a canoe in the middle of a river at midnight; arrangements are made for him to visit Omokachi to perform the rites. Back in Omokachi a celebratory dance is held. Afterwards Ihuoma and Ekwueme converse happily together, but she refuses to anticipate the marriage by sleeping with him. The following day Ekwueme presents Ihuoma with some meat and asks her to help in assembling the required ingredients for the coming sacrifice.

NOTES AND GLOSSARY:

cabalistic patterns: patterns traced for secret magical purposes

Chapter 30

Agwoturumbe arrives triumphantly in Omokachi. He orders Ekwueme to hire a canoe so that the sacrifice can be performed the same night. Ekwueme feels nervous about the rituals involved, but after reassurances from Agwoturumbe, he goes to the river and hires a boat from a boatman who expresses scepticism about the existence of the Sea-King. Returning to Ihuoma, he instructs her son, Nwonna, to shoot a brightly-coloured lizard in preparation for the sacrifice. He tells his wife-to-be that he will pay the bride-price on her the following day, when the rites are completed. They embrace happily. Stepping out of the door to check on Agwoturumbe's progress with the preparations, Ekwueme is shot in the stomach by a barbed arrow which Nwonna has fired at a lizard. Ihuoma and Adaku rave and moan as Agwoturumbe pulls out the bloody arrow-head. Ekwueme dies at midnight.

NOTES AND GLOSSARY:

rats' ears, mbelekuleku leaves: leaves of medicinal herbs

Part 3

Commentary

Subject and theme

When studying any literary work it is useful to make a distinction between subject matter and theme. Most literature of value possesses both subject and theme, and the act of defining them helps the reader in his appreciation of the text. Subject matter includes whatever the author is specifically dealing with—the material he has chosen to present to the reader or audience. Theme is more difficult to define, but it may be defined as the underlying principle or basic idea which the subject matter—situations, characters, dialogue, events—serves to illustrate, represent or embody. The detail in the subject matter will illustrate a deeper underlying statement which the writer is seeking to express. The value of the work of art is partly that it gives dramatisation to ideas or views of life which may not be our own, and helps to extend and deepen our human sympathies. The theme, therefore, is closely linked to the question of the author's intention. If we approach *The Concubine* in this light, what do we find?

First, subject matter. This could be placed under two headings, the specific and the general. Specifically, Amadi takes as his subject the career of Ihuoma. The limited subject might be expressed as Ihuoma's tragic impact upon the men of the village. A more general definition would be that Amadi deals with traditional village life in Africa. This may serve to distinguish *The Concubine* from some other novels we have read but it does not give a precise sense of the story. A full definition would be: the subject of *The Concubine* is the tragic outcome of Ihuoma's love affairs within a traditional African setting.

The theme may be approached in a similar way. On the first level the theme is the clash between the human and the supernatural. To support this reading we may quote the prefatory poem: 'The Thunder-god feasts in his grove, Then naps 'twixt rainbows up above; But justice suffers here below, And we know not which way to go'. The clash is most pronounced in the meting out of what seems unmerited suffering to Emenike, Ekwueme and Ihuoma; even Madume's punishment is surely excessive for his crime. Natural human emotions, motives, desires and actions are regularly viewed, not only from the human but from the religious point of view, and the narrative demonstrates that the gods do not conform to human sets of values. This suggests a simple determinism; that is, the idea that the whole action was pre-arranged by the gods, and the characters are simply puppets acting out their roles. There is a strong element of this in the novel; but if it were the whole truth then the tale of Ihuoma would be less moving and involving for the reader than it undoubtedly is. The second level of thematic material enriches this bare determinism, and is perhaps most clearly stated on page 127:

> Omokachi village life was noted for its tradition, propriety, and decorum. Excessive or fanatical feelings over anything were frowned upon and even described as crazy. Anyone who could not control his feelings was regarded as being unduly influenced by his agwu.

The last sentence refers, not to Ahurole, who is said to suffer the malign influence of her 'agwu', but to Ekwueme, who seeks to go against the sacred force of 'tradition, propriety, and decorum' with fatal results. Later on the same page it is said of Ihuoma that she 'behaved true to type' in accepting fate: 'She had had her chance and if the gods had been rather cruel there was nothing she could do about it'. These words are worth pondering deeply. They show us two opposing ways of reacting to the dictates of both society and the gods: acceptance of the communal good, or individualistic striving to alter 'fate'. The emphasis upon communal will is especially significant: if each person selfishly seeks his own ends, then the beautiful order of this society is threatened. Amadi deals with a theme that has been well defined by a fellow Nigerian writer, Wole Soyinka:

> Where society lives in a close inter-relation with Nature, regulates its existence by natural phenomena within the observable processes of continuity—ebb and tide, waxing and waning of the moon, rain and drought, planting and harvest—the highest moral order is seen as that which guarantees a parallel continuity of the species.*

The existence of Omokachi is founded in such a relationship with Nature. Its laws and etiquette are designed to foster that relationship, and its religion is directed to keeping destructive forces at bay. The unity and stability of the village are lovingly examined in the novel. Yet this cohesion may sometimes be bought at the expense of human happiness—this is hinted at, and because of the simplicity of language the reader should take care not to underestimate the richness of suggestion in the book. Amadi's aim is clearly enough to bring this traditional life into focus, and through the subtle deployment of his twin themes—the clash of man and the gods, and the occasional clash of group and personal identity—he draws the reader into this world of man and spirits.

*Wole Soyinka, *Myth, Literature and the African World*, Cambridge, Cambridge University Press 1978, p.52.

The Concubine recreates the African past in the present, and the people of the village are real: they suffer, enjoy life, entertain hopes, feel vulnerable.

It may be observed that the tragic differences between human and divine will are left unresolved by Amadi in terms of the realism of the novel. Do the gods exist in reality, or are they active purely as figments of the imagination of the people? The novelist shows that collective opinion and belief are not something outside ourselves. Omokachi is a collection of individuals who find in the idea of gods and ancestors what may be a collective illusion, but an illusion that makes for a peaceful, ordered society of considerable beauty and wisdom. Man, whether 'advanced' or 'primitive', appears to need the support of a religious system to explain the mystery of the universe in which he finds himself. If the fates of Ihuoma and her lovers are dealt with arbitrarily by the gods who preside over the great forests, the overall feeling of the book is one of lyrical celebration. In looking back to this communal world which is now lost forever, Amadi would seem to share with Chinua Achebe a desire to:

> teach my readers that their past—with all its imperfections—was not one long night of savagery from which the first Europeans acting on God's behalf delivered them.*

Story, plot, and narrator

We read a novel for a variety of reasons, but primarily for its story. The writer has a tale to tell and primarily he should make this interesting. The story will be the sum total of what happens in the novel—in this case everything that is done by Emenike, Ihuoma, Ekwueme and the rest of the characters. But does Amadi succeed in giving any coherence to the story, or is it just a random selection of incidents arranged in some sort of chronological order? This is where the concept of plot comes in: plot is the underlying pattern of causes which determines the action and keeps it moving ahead. Amadi's book is tightly-plotted; in one sense indeed everything stems from the opening fight—Emenike's death, Madume's suicide, Ihuoma's widowhood, Ekwueme's courtship and sudden death. This train of events is set in motion at the outset and the narrative runs forward to its inevitable outcome. The story of *The Concubine* is told chronologically: that is, it moves straight forward in time from start to finish, although within this framework the narrator allows himself 'deletions' (gaps in time sequence: for example, one year between Emenike's death and second burial; six months between

*Chinua Achebe, *Morning Yet on Creation Day*, Heinemann Educational, London 1975, p.45.

the marriage negotiations and Ahurole's arrival in Omokachi). No incident is described that is not related to this train of events, and each episode helps the narrative forward. The only exceptions are the two passages of 'flashback', accounts of events prior to the time of the action of the novel. The first of these, in Chapter 20, gives a sketch of Ekwueme's childhood which enables us to understand his present behaviour; the second, in Chapter 28, provides an explanation of Ihuoma's origins in the spirit world which sets the entire action in a new light and gives the story its title. Both episodes are necessary to the story, in furnishing background information, and to the plot, in accounting for causes hidden from the current narrative. The second flashback does more: it permits the reader an alternative way of reading the plot by giving the events a supernatural as well as a natural cause. The plot is beautifully articulated to bear either interpretation, and the narrator impartial in his account of causation.

This brings us to the teller of the tale. Story-telling is an ancient art which is founded in oral tradition. We may imagine such a tale as Ihuoma's being set as a ballad or folk tale and retold from generation to generation. The purpose of such types of narrative was to celebrate, to warn, to teach; but Amadi's purposes here may be more complex. The Russian novelist Tolstoy once observed that if 'all the complex lives of many people go on unconsciously, then such lives are as if they had never been'. Amadi here celebrates and records the lives of his ancestors in a realistic way. The 'realism' of the narrative, its persuasive selection of detail, is important in a story dealing with the intervention of supernatural forces in the human world. The rituals and sacrifices are recounted in a detailed matter-of-fact manner which shows that the characters accept such matters as part of everyday life. Thus what may seem exotic to the reader in the abstract becomes totally believable in the way it is presented by the narrator. Realism assumes that we are given a world which we recognise and can believe in whilst we are reading the text; even the seemingly incredible situations have a deep truth to reality, and the narrator's artful shaping of events makes it interesting and pleasurable for us to read about what would be painful to experience.

Through the story of Ihuoma and her relations with men, Amadi creates an organic world which is complete in itself; much of his success depends upon his skill and consistency as narrator. While studying *The Concubine* the student should pay close attention to the role of the narrator. Amadi does not ever present himself directly in the story; the tale is told by what we call 'the implied narrator', someone who is there telling the story, but whose presence we infer.

The unity of *The Concubine* derives not only from the small geographical scale but also from the careful manipulation of tone: that is, the writer's attitude to his subject matter and to his imagined audience. Amadi's characteristic tone is one of deep insight into an ancient social order. We can see this in the opening paragraph describing Emenike in the forest:

> He was aware that a venerable old chief had died somewhere. This death was kept as secret as possible. This was because they wanted to give the head-hunters who were now abroad in the forests a chance to capture heads for the great burial. One trapper had seen some of these fellows stalking in the forest and so word had gone round Omokachi that the forests were 'unhealthy'. But of course every man who was a man would go about his business, head-hunters or no. (p.1)

This passage illuminates narrative-procedure throughout the novel, which is a mixture of omniscient (all-seeing) and limited viewpoint. We are partly 'outside' Emenike and the description of the scene includes him as one component within it, as in a film scene—'He tightened his grip on his razor-sharp matchet', and so on; but we can also slide into his consciousness and share his attitudes—'of course every man who was a man . . .'. Amadi includes both direct narrative in the third person and free indirect speech which reproduces the characters' inner thoughts; in this way the narrator is able to reproduce both public and social, private and individual experience. If there is more dialogue than free indirect speech, this is because *The Concubine* deals with a co-operative public world. The easy style of the narrative has the flow of quiet conversation expressing deep familiarity with Omokachi society. An example of this is to be found in the portrait of Madume given in Chapter 2:

> It was very easy for him to pick quarrels with Emenike because many events called for a degree of intimacy between the villagers. Take the sharing of meat after a general village hunt. Madume would always argue that Emenike had not been particularly active in the killing of a particular animal and so deserved only a fraction of what the old men actually gave him. But Emenike was not afraid of him. He knew he could hold his own against him any day given a fair chance. But a man's god may be away on a journey on the day of an important fight and that may make all the difference. This was clearly what had happened in the last fight between Madume and Emenike. (p.5)

Here the narrator moves from objective presentation of Madume, through Emenike's feelings, to an expression of village opinion. There is no gap between the implied narrator and his characters, and the whole passage is couched in quiet conversational tones, as in 'Take the sharing of the meat . . .'. The voice of the narrator is that of one closely bound up with the imagined world he presents, sharing some of its values and opinions, as in this description of Ihuoma's farm:

> It was 'a home farm' as opposed to farms farther afield. It lay on one side of the path leading to the main farming area of the village. It was a hot afternoon but pear trees, palm wine trees and silk cotton trees provided adequate shade. That was a distinct advantage of a 'home farm'; it never lacked shady trees. (p.149)

In the final comment the narrator 'becomes' a villager. Elsewhere, on the contrary, he is careful to relay village opinion without comment, and the reader is left to fill in the interpretative gaps. He comments, for example, 'although it was clear that Emenike had died of "lock-chest", careful observers could not help noticing a link between the fight and his subsequent illness and death' (p.19). The reader must make up his own mind. A more extended instance is found in Chapter 11, where the narrator, having recounted Ekwueme's declaration of love for Ihuoma, gives no clue as to her reaction. At other times the narrator moves with assurance from objective description to psychological analysis of states of mind, as here, after the arbitration over Ekwueme's marriage:

> Ekwueme was annoyed with himself. Before marriage he thought he knew all the answers to domestic problems and vowed that when he got married he would never have to call in a third party, not even his parents, to decide anything between him and his wife. He used to despise men who had to beat their wives and call in arbitrators to settle disputes every other day. Now that he was one of them, he felt confused. (p.143)

The description of Ihuoma's reflections on Madume's death, as she is outwardly preoccupied with cracking nuts (p.77), or Ekwueme's excitement over Ihuoma (p.85), are other examples of this psychological realism. Elsewhere Amadi skilfully mingles dramatic realisation of character through dialogue with analysis of inner feeling, as in the conversation between Ekwueme and Ihuoma in Chapter 9 (see especially p.47). There are numerous examples, but the student should always be aware of the role of the narrator in mixing objective and subjective description, in altering the pace of the narrative at crucial points (for example, in the pursuit of Ekwueme in Chapter 25), or the piling up of incidental detail, as in the scenes of divination.

The realisation of character by the narrator is necessarily limited in *The Concubine*, because the novel deals with relatively unsophisticated people, who speak from a narrow experience of their own small world. Yet it is wrong to call them simple. Amadi's novel possesses real depth, even though he is bound by the plot to exclude a more 'advanced' character who might act as his mouthpiece, as is often done in novels of modern life. Such a mouthpiece could express ironic, questioning views which would be out of place in Omokachi where the people are totally bound up with the affairs of daily existence. The limits of the sceptical viewpoint are denoted in the peripheral figure of the boatman who harbours doubts about the existence of the Sea-King. The doubt is registered briefly, but soon overwhelmed by Ekwueme's deep-seated superstitious fears. The narrator creates characters not only through their appearance and habits, but also through the sympathy and understanding which he extends (and we through him) to this simpler world, and through the reaction of other characters. Indeed, Ihuoma's story is dominated by this sense of social reaction. Amadi shares his 'authority' as narrator with the characters, and especially with the communal voice of Omokachi village. The characters are varied enough to create a community of separate but connected people; for instance, reactions to Madume's assault on Ihuoma range from her own tearful outrage, through the angry efforts of the villagers to restrain him, to the later jocular composition of a song about the incident by Wodu and Ekwueme. The full 'truth' about a character or incident depends to a large extent therefore upon the point of view, and the narrator shifts and manipulates this within a consistent and unified overall perspective. Because the narrator clearly values the hearts and minds of the people he has created he deliberately plays down his own omniscience. His intimate and familiar understanding of the society must derive from acquaintance with people such as these, and from a deep-seated love of the traditional way of life recorded here.

Amadi has formed his view of life partly from contemplation of traditional experience, and at appropriate points in the narrative he delegates his authorial powers to characters who speak directly from this experience. The narrator of an apparently 'artless' tale like *The Concubine* must never be taken for granted by the reader: Amadi's is the art which conceals art, and the seemingly natural narrative flow is in fact the result of hard creative work and careful cultivation of viewpoint.

Style

The reader will experience few difficulties with Amadi's prose style; the writing is clear, graceful and direct. The Igbo novelists generally favour a quiet prose laced with proverbial sayings and other marks of traditional wisdom. This is a style in marked contrast to that of their fellow Nigerian writers in Yorubaland, who tend to use exaggerated rhetorical effects and complex syntax and vocabulary. It has been suggested that the two styles reflect different political systems, the direct democracy of the Igbo as against the Yoruba kingship hierarchy. However that may be, the reader can train himself to recognise different styles or modes of discourse within the overall simplicity of *The Concubine*. There is firstly a plain narrative style:

> Madume leaped for a flying tackle. His opponent sank on one knee, collected him on his shoulders and flung him heavily to the ground. Emenike disengaged himself and waited. He would not close in yet. Madume got up and decided to come to grips with his man. For several minutes they pushed each other about treading down bushes like antelopes caught in a rope trap. At last Madume got his two arms under his opponent's armpits and began to push him back at full speed hoping that some undergrowth would entangle his legs and make him fall. (p.2)

The construction here is based on a set of statements divided into simple clauses or sentences which progress in uninterrupted flow. Movement is at a premium, and the language is devoid of metaphor (implied comparison) or other figurative language, apart from one simile which is so closely related to the context of trapping that it does not interrupt the discourse. The total effect of such prose is of a bald but grand simplicity rather like the old sagas or Greek epics. In the many conversational scenes the language works to show the characters communicating lucidly and straightforwardly. The dialogue has the natural ease of talk between intimates. The shared communal life of Omokachi does away with the need for complicated verbal procedures, as so much is understood in ancestral memory. The simplicity is particularly telling in the fine scenes between Ihuoma and Ekwueme; here Amadi explores shifts and emotional undercurrents in a relationship which is not primarily verbal—the dialogue acts as a signal of the unspoken declarations being made at another level of being, as in the scene where Ekwueme declares he will pay the bride-price on Ihuoma (pp.89–90). The exchange has just the right mixture of familiarity and uncertainty: after all, the two have known each other a long time but now they are hovering on the brink of a new type of relationship. Both man and woman come before us with fine actuality.

The student should try to attune himself to Amadi's acute ear, and the way he is able to differentiate between speech-patterns according to social grouping. There is a difference, for example, between the boisterous talk of the young men and the proverbial lore which gives the elders their weight and dignity; or between the joking talk of Wodu and the banter of the young girls visiting Ahurole. Habits of language are cultural by-products, and extremely revealing of both character and social status. As examples of this the student may profitably compare the witty repartee of Ekwueme and Wodu, the quiet confidentiality of Ihuoma and Nnenda, and the broad, noisy teasing of Ahurole and Titi.

Amadi's prose is capable of other effects, and he adopts a heightened 'poetic' style where appropriate. These high points serve as contrast to the unforced tone of the main narrative. The most notable passage of this nature is the scene at the shrine in Chapter 4, where Amadi builds up the atmosphere with masterly precision:

> They talked less and less as they approached the Sacred Woods of Amadioha. Rank trees bordered the dark path. Some climbers were so thick they looked like ordinary trees. At the shrine absolute stillness reigned and it was quite cold as the high majestic roof of thick foliage, like a black rain cloud, cut off the sun completely. Even the wind could only play meekly among the undergrowth.
>
> The shrine was at the foot of a massive silk cotton tree. It was fenced off with a ring of tender palm shoots and their yellow colour blazed like a flame against the dark background. Nwokekoro went into the temple and placed some kola nuts in front of two carved figures clothed in blood and feathers. The floor of the shrine was ringed with earthenware pots each containing manillas, cowries, alligator pepper and feathers of animals many years old. There were skulls of animals on either side of the two carved figures. Emenike, who had never before been so close to the shrine, peered into the darkness and thought that one or two skulls looked human.
>
> When Nwokekoro came out of the shrine, he moved about so casually that one could not help feeling that somehow there was a great understanding between him and the god. He never hurried and yet he dispatched each part of the ceremony with precision. His face was almost expressionless, but there was an incomprehensible look about his eyes. Instead of looking outwards they seemed to be staring inwards into his head. Although he was obviously concentrating very hard, there was no rigidity about his features. . . [Emenike] gazed at the priest and immediately regretted that he had done so, for in the priest's face he read mild reproach, pity, awe, power, wisdom, love, life and—yes, he was sure—death. In a fraction of a second he relived his past life. In turns he felt deep affection for the priest and a desire to embrace him, and nauseating repulsion which made him want to scream with disgust. He felt the cold grip of despair, and the hollow sensation which precedes a great calamity; he felt a sickening nostalgia for an indistinct place he was sure he had never been to.
>
> He regained consciousness with a start. (pp.16–17)

Direct reportorial presentation at the outset, 'They talked less and less . . .' gives way to metaphorical description in which the natural scene signals an increase in tension and human apprehension: the 'rank trees', 'dark path', and 'absolute stillness', the absence of life-giving sun, and the transference effect of the wind playing '*meekly* among the undergrowth' (the meekness is really felt by the men approaching the shrine)—all of this combines to hint at the frightening power of the nature-gods, and man's relative insignificance in the scheme of things. After the darkness of the first paragraph the narrator invokes bright colours in the second; the yellow palm shoots which 'blazed like a flame' and the carved figures covered with blood—this marks the transition from natural surroundings to the shrine itself with its carefully catalogued, slightly sinister objects, and its hint of human sacrifice. The long third paragraph aptly reproduces both the mystic contemplation of the priest and Emenike's puzzled observance of that state, which crystallises into anticipation of his own death. The suddenness with which he pulls himself together is given by the single sentence standing alone, and then in the ensuing dialogue where the social intercourse once more replaces individual emotion. Setting, background or atmosphere here transcend the limitations such terms often imply; here they are determinants of the action.

Amadi's style, therefore, would be better termed Amadi's *styles*; careful reading of the text will help us to distinguish the variety of linguistic resource and the subtlety of verbal effects within *The Concubine*. Once again, the student will gain the most from close and repeated attention to the text.

Characterisation

While the student needs to identify the main characters and their place in the action, and to be able to describe them clearly and economically, he should never lose sight of their role in the narrative. The characters cannot be detached from the novel and any character analysis should take full account of the person's participation in the plot. When we attempt the exercise of writing on individual characters we do well to ponder some words of the American novelist Henry James (1843–1916): 'What is character but the determination of incident? What is incident but the illustration of character?' This is specially so in the African novel; whereas a European novel will often take as its central theme the development of an individual, the African novel of traditional life tends towards a portrait of an entire community. The form of such a novel is determined by rhythms appropriate to tribal existence—farming activities, religious festivals, music and dancing, and so on—rather than the essentially private events which often dominate the westernised novel. Thus in *The Concubine* we like and admire Ihuoma and Emenike, and watch Ekwueme's struggles sympathetically; but there is no single character by whom we are deeply moved. Instead Amadi deploys a range of skilfully distinguished individuals acting within a complex network of interdependence and connected by strong religious, social, and economic ties. A man born into Omokachi is born into an ancestral group. He is not just an individual, but has links with the living and dead of the clan. The community acts as the framework for the activities of the characters; there is no question of anyone in Omokachi 'going it alone'. For this reason Amadi's characterisation takes as its base the social definition of the person concerned: his or her profession (Anyika the dibia, Nwokekoro the priest, Mmam the drummer), or social status (Adaku's position as senior wife, Ihuoma's as widow, the seniority of the elders as a group). This type of characterisation gains its reality from its relationship with African village culture. The individual is conceived in terms of status or profession, family background, and ultimately his relationship with the gods and ancestors. As we read we can discern both this communal presentation and the real-life actions of the characters in themselves. That is, we come to see the people both as elements in a traditional culture and as human beings living in an identifiable society.

Madume

A blustering bully, never content with what he owns, Madume's function is to instigate the plot by challenging Emenike to a fight which weakens and in the last analysis kills him. He is of fierce appearance and strongly built, yet he is not particularly strong, and is often beaten at wrestling. He is lazy, refuses to re-thatch his roof, and mistreats his wife, blaming her for producing only daughters. His greed leads him into trouble, although he does have a conscience about Emenike's death. Later he decides he is not to blame and renews his claim to the disputed land and even to Ihuoma herself, with fatal results. His blindness reduces Madume to a pathetic state; for all his faults his suicide is a shocking event.

Emenike

Deliberately contrasted with Madume, he is regarded as the ideal young man by the elders and is a favourite with the girls. But he is also courageous, having descended from a family of braves. Despite these personal advantages he is modest and intelligent, and often employed on village missions. He is a devoted husband, as we see in the little dance scene. Like Madume he is in the grip of forces beyond his control, as he realises at the shrine.

Anyika

The village dibia is widely respected in Omokachi, but his origins are suitably mysterious. For the villagers he is vital as the mediator between them and the spirit world. He is called on at all the crises of the novel—Emenike's sickness, Madume's blindness and suicide, Ahurole's love-potion, Ekwueme's madness, and so on. He is a kindly man who is widely admired, and refuses to raise his hand against anyone in the village. Despite his prowess there are limits to his abilities: at the end he graciously makes way for the superior potency of an outside dibia.

Nnadi

Ihuoma's brother-in-law Nnadi acts as as her faithful protector after Emenike's death. He pays for the divination when Emenike is injured, gives Ihuoma assistance with the second burial rites, mends her roof, and watches over her interests.

Wodu Wakiri

Bringing gaiety, music and life into the village with his jokes and songs, an excellent dancer although he is small and knock-kneed, Wodu is always a welcome visitor. He takes an active part in village affairs, for example in thatching Ihuoma's roof, or the search party for Ekwueme. His jocular habits threaten to disturb the negotiations over Ahurole, but his good nature soon wins over her father. A staunch friend to Ekwueme, he feels baffled when faced with deep sorrow since he makes a joke of his own misfortunes. Yet his is capable of deep feelings, and when Ekwueme appears to be deranged he weeps.

Ahurole

One of the rare neurotics in the fiction of traditional life. She veers between high-spirited practical jokes and bouts of unexplained weeping. This is ascribed to her 'agwu', a minor Igbo spirit which takes possession of those marked out for religious or artistic roles. Because she is not assigned such a role she behaves unconventionally. When he sees the shyness and defiance mingled in her face, Ekwueme realises the marriage will be stormy, and so it proves. Although Ekwueme's mother-complex is to blame for much of the marital trouble, Ahurole's fits of moodiness make her a wholly unsuitable marriage partner for him. She foolishly adopts her mother's suggestion of the love-potion, and when the results prove disastrous she leaves the village in disgrace.

Wigwe

Ekwueme's father plays a crucial role in the story. His relationship with his son is one of mutual respect, though Ekwueme is prepared to thwart his father if need be. Such an occasion is the proposed marriage to Ahurole. Wigwe knows his clever strategem in calling on Ihuoma is contemptible, but his primary duty is to get the best wife for his son, and to avoid the disgrace of abandoning a childhood betrothal. His motives are good but his action is blameworthy. He is like his son in wanting his own way, and refusing to be dictated to. Later Wigwe is distressed by Ekwueme's collapse, and ages quickly. Although he is deeply grateful to Ihuoma for her help in speeding his son's recovery, as a member of the older generation he is alarmed at the revelation of her supernatural origins.

Ekwueme

An only child for almost twelve years, Ekwueme bears the marks of one who has been spoilt and cosseted. Despite Wigwe's entreaties, Adaku gave all her attention to the boy. As a result he grew up slow and clumsy, and was at first mocked by other boys. A stroke of luck gave him a reputation as a fighter, and he soon joined in wrestling, hunting and other manly pursuits. But everything he does is still motivated by a desire to please his mother, with whom he enjoys an intimate relationship. He is afraid of other women, and his love for Ihuoma develops out of a desire for a mother-figure. He does not know how to approach so mature and distinguished a young woman, and feels hurt by her rebuffs. Because he is used to having his own way he tries to kick against tradition by refusing to honour the betrothal to Ahurole. When crossed he can be quick-tempered, as we see when, returning home rebuffed by Ihuoma he turns angrily on his mother and sister (pp.48–9).

Ekwueme, however, is essentially an attractive and lively young man, fond of jokes, and imbued with a very musical spirit. Defeated by his father's ruse he enters into marriage 'like a sleep-walker', and soon becomes indifferent to his difficult young bride. As Wigwe justly observes, Ekwueme wishes to 'make a mother of his wife'. When he fails he feels isolated, and under the influence of the love-potion becomes unbalanced for a while. The onset of his madness is finely rendered by Amadi; we share the suspense, the misery of his parents, and the communal fear of losing a third young man so soon. We sympathise with Ekwueme's plight here, whilst recognising its source in his mother-complex. His deepening love for Ihuoma enables him to shake off his mother's influence; towards the close of the book Ekwueme emerges happier and more fulfilled. But the irony dominating the supernatural action it is at this moment of hope that Ekwueme is cut down.

Ihuoma

In the portrait of Ihuoma Amadi succeeds in one of the most difficult feats for a novelist: to make a wholly good person interesting for the reader. Ihuoma is a very beautiful young woman, but although conscious of her attractions, she resists all temptations to arrogance or egotism. On the contrary she is 'sympathetic, gentle, and reserved'. Her selflessness is demonstrated by her ministrations to Emenike, and later to Ekwueme. Ihuoma does not have an icy perfection; when Wolu (whose husband has effectively killed Emenike) comes to call, Ihuoma's first impulse is to reprimand her bitterly, but her gentler nature prevails. She exercises similar discretion during Wigwe's ill-advised visit.

Her self-control is remarkable, and she appears perhaps a little too perfect at the outset. But the portrayal develops our sense of Ihuoma's warm humanity, and we see her true feelings beginning to well up to the surface—as in her dream of Emenike, or her distress after Wigwe's visit and her subsequent anger with Nwonna. The upsurge of emotion in her is held in check by her highly developed sense of communal duty and responsibility. This sense enables her to fulfil such functions as her husband's second burial, or visit of welcome to Ahurole, with complete aplomb. She bears the isolation of widowhood nobly and is universally admired. But her reputation as one of the best women in Omokachi becomes a strait-jacket and threatens to destroy her hopes of individual happiness: 'She became less delighted when people praised her. It was as if they were confining her to an ever-narrowing prison' (p.153). She finally escapes from this 'prison' through the love of Ekwueme, which she comes to reciprocate. Ihuoma now attains a new-found happiness and serenity, a radiant new beauty. The revelation of her true origin as a goddess from the spirit world intervenes and crushes her last opportunity of personal fulfilment. As the concubine she is destined never to know married love on earth.

A detailed commentary

Chapter 1

In this highly economical presentation, no descriptive background information is given: the entire action stems from the opening scene. We are introduced to a 'primitive' society—the first paragraph indicates that head-hunting is still practised, and this is mentioned again when Emenike visits the shrine. The narrator's voice implies his intimacy with the lives of trappers and palm-wine tappers. Distinction between the young men is well made: Madume ugly and quarrelsome, Emenike good-looking and graceful. The fight signals the main concern of the novel, since one of Madume's motives is jealousy over Ihuoma.

NOTE:

(*a*) hints that the men are being 'trapped' by the wife of the Sea-King in description of the two fighting 'like antelopes caught in a rope trap' (p.2); the image is repeated later (p.16).

(*b*) the significance of the tree-stump; trees were important in African religions, and it may be no coincidence that Madume is later blinded by a snake in a tree, and that the deranged Ekwueme takes refuge in a tree, having earlier retrieved his boyhood reputation by pushing a boy over a tree-stump.

Chapter 2

This shows how a jealous man can cause trouble in a close-knit community. Reliance upon the dibia reveals both the society's reliance on superstition and Ihuoma's love for her husband.

NOTE:

The village belief that 'a man could not wrestle with a god' (p.9), a belief borne out in the careers of all three men.

Chapter 3

A careful delineation of Ihuoma's character and appearance. Amadi wishes to show the young couple and their children as a happy family unit so as to emphasise more firmly the distress caused by Emenike's sudden death.

NOTE:

(*a*) the preparation for future developments: when Ihuoma sits watching the lizards playing (p.10); and later references to Nwonna with his bow and arrows (for example p.83).

(*b*) the song composed to ridicule a married woman (p.12): personal behaviour is regulated by society, as Ihuoma feels to her cost later; this woman is contrasted with the goodness of Ihuoma.

Chapter 4

This stresses the local nature of the action, which is to be confined to Omokachi with its attendant gods.

NOTE:

Anticipation in the comment that 'Madume's "big eye" may cost him his life eventually' (p.16).

Chapter 5

Emenike's death is announced with deliberate bluntness—the arbitrariness of life, and man's dependence on the whim of the gods is thus suggested. Ihuoma's gentle nature is brought out in interviews with Wolu and her own mother. Ekwueme is introduced without comment. His advice, to trust in the will of the gods, is highly ironic in view of what is to happen later.

NOTE:

(*a*) the image of Emenike's grave as a 'big red boil on a black skin' (p.19); this is echoed later: other characters suffer boils (p.61), including Ekwueme, Emenike's successor (p.162)—a hint that there is some evil abroad in the community.

(*b*) 'What would other women think of her?' (p.19): Wolu's visit to Ihuoma is dictated by social pressure.

(*c*) 'Amadioha will kill them . . .' (p.20): a presentiment of Madume's death.

Chapter 6

The direction of the narrative is suggested by Ekwueme's annoyance that Ihuoma should suffer protracted widowhood. The man's qualities are sketched in: he is a good friend, and very musical. The dance scene emphasises the communal shared life of the villagers, and way they are connected by deep unspoken feelings and traditions. Ihuoma's dream, the first of several in the novel, shows that Emenike is not settled in the spirit world, and that she feels his loss keenly. The dance compares sadly with Ihuoma's earlier private dance of joy.

Chapter 7

The completion of second burial rites for Emenike ends the first section of the plot, and the new direction dictated by Ekwueme's courtship is indicated when Ihuoma ironically asks Nnenda, 'Who is admiring me?'. This new movement is imaged in nature: after the rains the farms are 'blooming'. But Ihuoma's wistful comment that beauty is associated with sorrow is borne out later.

Chapter 8

This focuses upon Ihuoma: her beauty and isolation are emphasised by contact with her family; the narrator ensures that we sympathise with the heroine here.

Chapter 9

The thatching scene shows how the community acts to support those in need. The delicate scene between Ihuoma and Ekwueme is beautifully rendered, and we note the contrast between female experience and male innocence.

NOTE:

(*a*) Ekwueme's dream, in which he is dragged across a stream by Emenike and others, may refer to the operations of the Sea-King.

(*b*) Ekwueme's hunting of the antelope can be seen as a metaphor for his approach to Ihuoma: initially he assumes he has caught it with little effort, but later he finds he has to employ all his guile to capture it.

Chapter 10

Madume feels free to 'pluck the various fruit trees on the land in dispute' (p.53)—a veiled reference to his desire to possess the fruitful Ihuoma. His attitude to his wife is stupid and selfish, and the approach to Ihuoma and the injury to his foot indicate trouble ahead. There is tragic irony in Anyika's remark that Madume can see 'with only two eyes' (p.60). We see how even a strong man like Madume is wholly subdued by the power of superstition.

NOTE:

The preparation for Madume's fate: the dibia tells him he is threatened by spirits from the sea, and when he sees Emenike's grave he shivers fearfully.

Chapter 11

Intimate communal life on the farms is stressed. Ekwueme's eagerness for Ihuoma is demonstrably immature at this stage—he has to earn the right to her hand.

Chapter 12

This is an excellent example of narrative pacing, in the quarrel and the snake's attack on Madume. The cause of Madume's rapid deterioration is left open—is it chance he has met the snake, or (as the dibia will reveal later) through the agency of the gods? The shock ending of the chapter, with Madume's suicide framed by the dance preparations, balances the shock opening of Chapter 5.

Chapter 13

Innocent chatter between the young women gives way to the main theme of Ekwueme's love for Ihuoma. The dialogue on page 80 is crucial—simple language reveals hidden depths, and the talk finally lapses into silence emphasised by the sound of Ihuoma's hammer.

NOTE:
The children catch a grasshopper and feed it piece by piece to the ants (p.83): an image expressive of the relations of the gods to man.

Chapter 14

Ekwueme appears more resolute here, but as soon as he is rebuffed he reacts childlishly. The existence of Ahurole is announced rather suddenly. Ihuoma is clear on social etiquette, and comments that to break a childhood engagement is to 'bring nothing but shame'—personal happiness is to be weighed against the rights and demands of the entire village. Yet we retain our sympathy for Ekwueme; after all, Ihuoma *is* vastly superior to Ahurole.

Chapter 15

The contrast between Ihuoma and Ahurole develops in the scene between Ahurole and Titi, who are lighthearted and flippant. Tradition dominates all the marriage negotiations. In the closing conversation, the women seem credulous and dependent on the male for information; in addition, the belief in the power of the Wakanchis tells us how blurred is the villagers' concept of life beyond the radius of their own community.

Chapter 16

Ekwueme now recognises that he is causing a serious crisis. But he is determined to have his own way, as he did when a boy. With hindsight we may notice Adaku's remark that it would be a mistake to marry Ihuoma (p.105). The difficulties in the traditional father-son relationship are exposed by Ekwueme's unacceptable display of independence.

Chapter 17

Wigwe's devious visit to Ihuoma takes the action further, and exposes Ekwueme's callowness and Ihuoma's vulnerability. Arguments between the mother and son emphasise the frustrations in Ihuoma's present state.

Chapter 18

The opening of negotiations for Ahurole begin Ekwueme's education into adult life, and he rightly foresees difficulties with Ahurole. Ihuoma's call on Ahurole shows how propriety outweighs personal feelings, and this emphasis is further developed in the following chapter.

Chapter 20

This chapter comprises a long analysis of Ekwueme's boyhood dependence on his mother, which is illustrated by him still hankering after her foo-foo even though he is now a married man.

Chapter 21

The disintegration of the marriage is expertly portrayed; we see Ekwueme increasingly cut off from his society and fantasising about Ihuoma, until tension breaks out in his fight with Ahurole.

Chapter 22

Notice how society accepts and even institutionalises the village madman; but Ekwueme feels more cut off than the madman, and is enveloped in an 'oppressive blanket of sadness'. In trying to avert Ekwueme's attentions, Ihuoma's motives are primarily social—she does not wish to be seen interfering in the marriage. But she begins to feel the constraints of her own position.

Chapter 23

Between Ahurole and Ekwueme explosive emotions arise over the trivial matter of the lost goat. The love-potion episode indicates an unacceptable attempt to tamper with human emotion.

Chapter 24

The effects of the love-potion are immediate and dramatic, but in a sense simply an acting out of what was an unsatisfactory situation.

Chapter 25

Violent action ensues in Ekwueme's flight; the split between man and wife is symbolised in the collision in the forest and Ekwueme's breaking the water-pot.

Chapter 26

This is a telling scene with Ekwueme removed from the village community, up the tree—a fine image of the gap that has arisen between him and his society. There is a striking effect of stillness when he descends the tree and 'nothing was heard but the cluck, cluck, cluck of a hen feeding her brood of chickens hard by' (p.181): the kindly family act in the animal world contrasts with the public break-up of Ekwueme's marriage.

Chapter 27

Ekwueme's love has gone too far and reduces him to a shadow of his former self. The 'magical' aspect of Ihuoma is hinted at when the narrator remarks that she has 'absolute power' over Ekwueme. Dialogue here has a natural ease and rhythm.

NOTE:
Ekwueme's eyes are 'drained of most of their intelligence'; compare this with 'big-eyed' Madume who is blinded; with Ihuoma's doubts as to whether Amadioha was 'not blind at least part of the time' (p.21); and references to Wodu Wakiri's 'large eyes' (e.g. pp.8, 171).

Chapter 28

Ihuoma begins to blossom under Ekwueme's love and can now ignore gossip. But while marriage plans proceed, the dibia sounds the note of warning: forces beyond the human are still dominant in the world of Omokachi. The entire action of the novel is suddenly thrown into a new light by the dibia's explanation. Ekwueme, headstrong as ever, determines to outface ancient wisdom, and the machinery for the final catastrophe is thus set up.

Chapter 29

The self-confidence of the dibia contrasts with the human doubts of Ekwueme. The pleasant interlude between Ihuoma and her lover acts as contrast with the dark events to come.

Chapter 30

The final chapter is crowded with details of life, but ends suddenly in death. Alternative views of life are presented by the dibia, spokesman of the supernatural, and the boatman, a sceptic who ascribes everything to natural agencies. Ekwueme feels hopelessly caught between these two alternatives, and after his shocking death the reader is left to determine the 'true' cause of the tragedy. The final scene is gripping in its awful simplicity.

NOTE:
The prefiguration in Ekwueme's remark that 'Tomorrow seems so far away' (p.213).

Part 4

Hints for study

THE NEED FOR the student to read *The Concubine* closely and repeatedly cannot be overstressed. It is always a difficult matter to remember all the necessary details of plot, dialogue and character, but such knowledge is essential if the student is to avoid writing vague, over-generalised essays on the novel. In re-reading we often come across points of detail, theme, image or character which we have not noticed before, and which make more sense when we have the entire structure clearly in our minds. Whilst the student cannot be expected to learn many quotations, as he might when studying poetry, he certainly will be expected to display a detailed command of the novel in all its aspects. Scrappy and superficial acquaintance with the text is not acceptable to examiners; *The Concubine* is, after all, a short and relatively simple novel, so that constant revision is perfectly feasible. By frequent re-reading and by making summaries of key chapters, a close working knowledge can soon be acquired.

As the student re-reads he should begin to make notes of important points in the narrative which are likely to relate to the type of question to be expected on *The Concubine*. When preparing to answer such questions the student should study the terms of the question very carefully at the outset. There will normally be questions about: (*a*) themes, (*b*) characters and (*c*) context.

In all cases the student should pay attention to the construction of his essay, and the presentation of material along the following lines:

(*a*) opening paragraph discussing the meaning and implications of the question and possible ways of treating it

(*b*) development section: a coherent treatment of the question with relevant detailed reference to the text

(*c*) conclusion: a section summing up what you have to say; essentially re-statement, and not including much new material.

While in questions about literature there are really no right or wrong answers in accordance with objective criteria, there are common faults which the students should avoid:

(*a*) re-telling the plot. This is a very common practice which wastes the time of both student and examiner; no question will ever demand a simple account of the story.

(*b*) treating a question about theme as a character-study; this is also common, and produces a largely irrelevant answer.

(*c*) misunderstanding or evading the question; questions should be read very carefully, since careless reading often leads students into serious misunderstanding of its implications; equally, avoid writing out a 'prepared' answer.

A key to topics, themes and characters

Superstition, magic, ritual

Fear of the forest (p.1); rites of purification for murder (p.3); Anyika's origins, and divination for Emenike (pp.5–7); sacred stream of Mini Wekwu (pp.14–15, 161); the gods (p.15); shrine of Amadioha (pp.15–18); Madume's consultation, and sacrifices (pp.58–60); Ahurole's love-potion (pp.159–61); divination of Ihuoma's origins (pp.195–6); Agwoturumbe (pp.199–200, 206 ff.).

Farming and other communal activities

Madume's failure as farmer (p.4); the elders discuss the harvest (p.16); thatching Ihuoma's roof (pp.42–6); friendly familiarity on the farms (p.64); dispute over plantains (pp.68–70); tying up the yams for Ihuoma (pp.87–9); the riverside market and rivalry with the Rikwos (p.145).

Humour

Good-humoured banter between Ihuoma, Emenike and the children (p.10); Wodu's jokes whilst thatching (pp.44–6); boy imitates his mother's voice (p.64); Wodu at yam tying (pp.87–8); Wodu's humour out of place in marriage discussions (p.118); Ekwueme, though sad, jokes with Ihuoma (p.146).

Music and dance

Oduma music to which Ihuoma dances secretly (pp.12–13); dance and song commemorating the dead Emenike (pp.26–8); the 'dance of anger' at Emenike's second burial (p.33); songs after the thatching (pp.44–5); dance preparations interrupted by discovery of Madume's corpse (pp.74–6); spontaneous dance with new song (p.86); Ahurole's marriage feast (p.123); Ihuoma joins a dance night (p.128); Wodu and Ekwueme sing to forget their sorrows (pp.156–7).

Setting

The general topography of the village and surrounding area (p.14).

Chance, fate

Prefatory poem; Ahurole sitting in 'unlucky' position (p.97); 'it would be a terrible mistake to marry Ihuoma'—Adaku (p.105); Ekwueme decides to depend on luck (p.109); how luck enabled the young Ekwueme to be thought a good fighter (p.131); Ekwueme feels it was bad luck to have married Ahurole (p.140).

Duty

Wolu's unpleasant duty in visiting the widowed Ihuoma (p.20); Ihuoma's sense of duty over second burial, and Nnadi's in helping her (pp.30–1); Ihuoma's determination to tend Emenike's compound (pp.92, 113); Wigwe's idea that his sole duty is to get a wife for his son (p.102); Ekwueme's realisation that he is causing a serious crisis by failing to do his duty and marry Ahurole (p.104); Nnadi acts up to the accepted code of conduct (p.112); Anyika's sense of duty will not allow him to harm the villagers (p.159); shock of Ekwueme turning down childhood engagement (p.177); Wigwe's primary duty to his son (p.117); Ihuoma would rather die than be thought a husband-snatcher (p.148); Ekwueme when mad fails to greet his elders dutifully (p.163).

Dreams and portents

The owl hoots eerily during divination for the injured Emenike (p.6); the dead Emenike appears to Ihuoma in a dream (pp.28–9); Ekwueme dreams he is lured across a stream (p.50); Nnenda's husband 'shot' in a dream (p.62).

Cooking and eating

Feast at the second burial (pp.31–3); meal at Ihuoma's parents and discussion of Ekwueme (pp.37–41); feast after thatching (pp.45–6); soup after tying up the yams (p.88); Ahurole quarrels with her brother over a meal (p.97); Ahurole's wedding feast (p.123); Ekwueme's childish devotion to his mother's foo-foo (p.130).

Characters

Madume: his lack of success (pp.4–5); greedy (p.53); fear of spirits (pp.58–60); changed nature after being blinded (p.71); suicide (p.76).

Emenike: good-looking and admired (p.5); good-humoured (p.10); love for wife (p.13).

Ahurole: difficulties with her agwu (Chapter 15); shyness and defiance (p.119); avoidance of Ekwueme (Chapter 18); high-spirited and tomboyish (p.137); guilt and misery after the love-potion (p.169).

Ihuoma: perfection and attractions (pp.10–12); forbearance in distress (pp.20–1); sadness (p.28); sorrow adds to her beauty (p.36); loneliness and sorrow after Wigwe's visit, and anger with her son (pp.115–6); worried and confused by Ekwueme's persistent attentions (p.152); radiant beauty in her love for Ekwueme (p.192).

Ekwueme: diffidence with Ihuoma (pp.47–8); anger with mother (pp.48–9); anxiety over Ihuoma (Chapter 11); finds Ihuoma incomprehensible (p.91); relations with father (p.106); tried to disguise boyishness when married (p.130); his ideal woman (p.138); becomes indifferent to Ahurole (p.138); changes for the worse under the love-potion (p.163); determination to marry the 'fatal' Ihuoma (p.197); fear of the divination (p.199).

Useful quotations

Death is a bad reaper, often plucking the unripe fruit. (p.34)
Beauty seems to carry sorrow with it. (p.35)
People did not just die without reason. Invariably they died either because they had done something wrong or because they had neglected to minister to the gods or to the spirits of their ancestors. (p.53)
It was impossible for the wicked to go unpunished. (p.77)
'... You are merely a woman but your good behaviour has placed you a little above many other women in the village'.—Wigwe to Ihuoma (p.112)
Propriety in the village often outweighed personal emotional conflicts. (p.125)
Omokachi village life was noted for its tradition, propriety, and decorum. Excessive or fanatical feelings over anything were frowned upon and even described as crazy. (p.127)
... Trying to make a mother of his wife.—Ekwueme (p.139)
She was something of a phenomenon. But she alone knew her internal struggles. She knew she was not better than anyone else. She thought her virtues were the products of chance. As the days went by she began to loathe her so-called good manners. She became less delighted when people praised her. It was as if they were confining her to an ever-narrowing prison.—Ihuoma (p.153)

Specimen questions

(1) It is sometimes said that Ihuoma is 'too good to be true'. Do you think this is a valid assessment of her character?

(2) Is *The Concubine* a suitable title for the book?

(3) '*The Concubine* will be remembered for its projection of an idyllic vision of traditional society, rather than for its depiction of human relationships.' Do you think this comment is justified?

(4) Discuss the part played by music and dancing in *The Concubine*.

(5) The series of deaths in *The Concubine* may be accounted for in various ways: natural causes, flaws in character, chance, or the retribution of the gods. How does Amadi reconcile these seemingly contradictory explanations?

(6) 'Ekwueme is too weak a character to make a successful hero.' Analyse the character and role of Ekwueme in the light of this remark.

(7) It has been said that we should not judge a novel dealing with the supernatural by our own feelings about its rationality or otherwise. Discuss the role which belief in the supernatural plays in *The Concubine* with this comment in mind.

(8) Analyse the part played by any *three* of the following in the novel: (*i*) dreams; (*ii*) eating and drinking; (*iii*) courtship; (*iv*) parenthood; (*v*) magic.

(9) Would you describe *The Concubine* as a love story?

(10) Amadi has been praised for his 'great delicacy' in his portrayal of human relationships in *The Concubine*. Do you think this praise justified? Illustrate your answer by close reference to any three of the following relationships: (*i*) Ihuoma and Emenike; (*ii*) Ekwueme and Ihuoma; (*iii*) Ekwueme and Wigwe; (*iv*) Ekwueme and Ahurole; (*v*) Ihuoma and Nnenda; (*vi*) Adaku and Ekwueme; (*vii*) Madume and Wolu.

(11) Read the following passage carefully and answer these questions: (*i*) Relate the passage briefly to its context. (*ii*) What kind of relationship is portrayed here? (*iii*) What does the scene contribute to the novel in terms of theme and character-portrayal?
(*iv*) How does the scene forward the development of the plot?

Ihuoma went home feeling worried. She had hoped that Ekwueme would in time forget about her. It now looked as if she was mistaken. She saw clearly that he was letting himself go and racked her brain for a way to keep him off. She was dismayed to find Ekwueme by her side at the cocoyam farm the next day. She thought of the number of passers-by who had seen them together during the past two days and her heart sank. In her desperation she found her tongue.

'Ekwe,' she said, 'why do you keep coming here? I am sure you are aware of the impression you are creating.'
'You are too particular, Ihuoma. What is wrong with us chatting together here?'
'You are bringing ridicule on me.'
'You are above any form of ridicule, Ihuoma.'
'You are married to my village girl. If she gets the impression that you are over-interested in me she will tell her parents and what type of figure will I cut at Omigwe?' Ekwueme was silent. He was cutting a pattern on the tree trunk with his matchet.
'Ekwe, please go away,' Ihuoma insisted. 'Go, go, please go.'
Adaku came by and Ekwe just managed to hide away. She greeted Ihuoma and passed.
'Now you see what I mean,' Ihuoma said when Ekwueme emerged once again. (p.151)

Model answers

(1) It is sometimes said that Ihuoma is 'too good to be true'. Do you think this is a valid assessment of her character?

The implication of the question centres on belief: it suggests that we do not find the portrayal of Ihuoma *credible* enough because she thinks and acts too perfectly. It is often the case in literature that we prefer to read about a character with human failings, with whom we sympathise, rather than about a character whose very perfection makes him somewhat repellent. We prefer a character whose motives are mixed to one who is either flawlessly good or wholly evil, because our experience confirms that most people have good and bad qualities within them. There is no inherent reason why a good person should not be interesting; the author's difficulty is to gain the reader's sympathy for his creation. Amadi, in fact, succeeds well in delineating a perfectly-behaved character who succeeds in engaging the sympathy of the reader, and we shall now examine how he achieves this.

First, there can be no doubt about Ihuoma's goodness. From the first moment that we see her tending the injured Emenike, to the last page where she grieves bitterly for the dying Ekwueme, she behaves without fault. When Emenike is ill she nurses him, when he recovers she dances for joy, and when he dies she is numb with distress. We cannot doubt her devotion to her first husband, dramatised by the second burial, and her determination to guard and care for her compound. Although we see less of her feelings for her three children, the indications are that she also centres her life selflessly on them—the only exception is her angry reprimand to Nwonna which comes as a reflex action to the insulting visit of Wigwe. The narrator stresses that Ihuoma's is not simply a passive goodness: she exerts all her efforts, for example, in farming Emenike's land after his death, in keeping his compound in good order, and in joining in communal activities. She is always helpful; she mediates in the quarrels of older women and does her utmost to aid the recovery of Ekwueme, despite the problems she has had with his family.

The keynote of Ihuoma's behaviour during her long and trying widowhood is restraint. As a young and exceedingly beautiful woman she is exposed to temptations and difficulties over which she triumphs. Although she likes Ekwueme, and needs the love and attention of a husband, she firmly rejects his advances so that he should remain true to his childhood engagement. When Ahurole settles in the village, Ihuoma readily visits her and tenders her good advice. As the marriage disintegrates she is worried by Ekwueme's renewed attentions and, despite her own disturbed emotional state, begs him to desist, saying she does not wish to be branded as a 'husband-snatcher'. Her behaviour is dictated not simply by personal emotion and desire, as is the case with other characters (for example, Madume or Ekwueme); the keynote to Ihuoma's character is her sense of *duty*, both to the community at large and to the ancestral gods. Whatever her sufferings she will not complain or take selfish action that would disrupt the order of village morality. She behaves 'true to type' as the narrator remarks, and will do nothing to upset this 'perfect setting'. The irony is that, as the dibia ultimately reveals, as a denizen of the spirit world Ihuoma is unwittingly disruptive.

Yet if self-denial is a significant element in Ihuoma's determination to observe the proprieties, she is neither an icily perfect martyr nor a boastful egotist about her goodness. Increasingly through the novel her inner doubts, conflicts and difficulties are revealed, and her loneliness comes to seem to her too high a price to pay for the good reputation she enjoys. To talk of Ihuoma's 'goodness' is therefore misleading since she suffers and feels conflicting human stresses. As examples we may cite her disturbing dream about Emenike, and feelings of sorrow and futility after his death; her anger with Wolu, which she suppresses only to give way to grief; her annoyance at her mother's proposal of Ekwueme as a suitor, and so on. On a larger scale her grave maturity in the developing relationship with Ekwueme masks a heart which is seeking love and companionship, but is confused and lonely. The result of this inner tension is that Ihuoma becomes understandably impatient with the good reputation which seems to be 'confining her to an ever-narrowing prison'. When, after Ekwueme's madness, she finally feels free to acknowledge and reciprocate his love, she achieves a 'new radiant form of beauty': her virtues, the reader feels, have gained their just reward, but one that is snatched away at the last.

Ihuoma, therefore, although she is fundamentally a good person, is by no means 'too good to be true'. If she has emerged from the perfection of the spirit world, then she certainly takes on full humanity as the story progresses. Her supposed role as water-goddess (a common enough legend in the riverine area of south-east Nigeria) is soon displaced by her actual human roles as lover, wife and mother. Her goodness is a matter of individual striving, of a conscious effort to balance public and private values and aspirations. Ihuoma ultimately impresses the reader as a very vulnerable human being in whom the desire to achieve goodness in society is counterbalanced by natural and credible human problems and feelings. That Ihuoma's final attainment of happiness is brutally cut short is no small part of the shattering effect of the final tragedy.

---

(2) Read the following passage carefully and answer these questions: (*i*) Refer the passage briefly to its context in the novel. (*ii*) What type of society is portrayed here? (*iii*) Comment on the style of the passage. (*iv*) What does this scene contribute to the development of the novel?

> Nnadi picked up his matchet which he had left leaning against the wall, and disappeared into the darkness shutting the door behind him. He knew it would be mean to inject himself into a conference to which he was not invited. He had acted up to the accepted code of conduct. But his coming made Wigwe think again. He had come to find out from Ihuoma whether his son had proposed to her and if so what her answer was. Nnadi's arrival reminded him forcibly that such a procedure was improper without Ihuoma's people being around. He realised he had no right to question her that way. It would appear he was taking undue advantage of her widowhood. It was persecution. Nnadi would certainly be angry if he knew about it later on.
>
> What then? He could not go back without saying something. For a time his mind was in a whirl. The silence grew distressing.
>
> 'Ihuoma, my child,' Wigwe began at last, 'really I ought to have come here with more people, but I have avoided formalities because I want to spare myself any embarrassments. Formalities will come later if all goes well. Please don't blame me.'
>
> Ihuoma, not knowing exactly what was coming this time, had no comments to make. She sat upright and directed her gaze meekly to the floor. That was the correct posture to adopt when being spoken to by an elder. She was desperately trying to be as blameless as possible in what was threatening to be a complicated state of affairs.

(*i*) This scene occurs in the middle of the novel. The evening visit of Wigwe and Ekwueme is prompted by the latter's refusal to honour his childhood betrothal to Ahurole and his insistence that he loves only

Ihuoma. Wigwe uses the visit as a ploy: he knows that Ihuoma is bound to refuse his son because of her widowhood, and that Ekwueme can then be compelled to go through with the negotiations over Ahurole.

(*ii*) This passage is replete with evidence as to the nature of the society portrayed. First, the act of Nnadi in picking up his matchet indicates a rural farming community. The remainder of the passage emphasises the traditional aspects of that rual society. Each person here clearly has a defined role; it is an ordered, hierarchical social arrangement with strict laws of conduct. Thus, Nnadi, Ihuoma's protective brother-in-law, acts in accordance with the 'accepted code' by checking that Ihuoma's visitors mean her no harm. Ihuoma equally behaves irreproachably, despite her misgivings as to the complications that this visit will entail. Ironically enough the one person to transgress the social code is Wigwe, an elder who should know better. The scene describes people in a society conservative and orthodox in its regulation of behaviour and personal feelings, in which wisdom and authority are highly honoured (as witness the humble attitude to be adopted by those addressed by an elder). But the order and decorum of this society is threatened by Ekwueme's assertion of self: it is this which causes Wigwe, his mind 'in a whirl', to persecute Ihuoma. Ultimately his aim is in fact to strengthen and uphold traditional values threatened here by a younger generation.

(*iii*) The style of narration is simple and direct, and both description and dialogue move swiftly and with no embellishment or unnecessary detail which might slow down the pace. The first paragraph consists of short staccato sentences—'He had acted up to the accepted code of conduct. But his coming made Wigwe think again.' This aptly reproduces action and thought-process of people certain of their role within a highly structured social order, and it betrays a society which places a premium on action rather than contemplation. The only exception is the description of Wigwe, who is so confused by the unaccustomed role he has to play that there is a prolonged silence of hesitation. When he does speak he expresses himself in rather long, repetitive sentences as if he is playing for time. The language is devoid of figurative expressions or imagery; the result is a clear, definite and fast-moving style which can still encompass doubt and conflicts of motive.

(*iv*) The scene is a key link in the chain of events running from Emenike's death to that of Ekwueme himself, a silent spectator here. By compelling Ekwueme to marry the immature Ahurole, Wigwe is creating a recipe for disaster and leaving open the possibility of Ekwueme returning to Ihuoma eventually. Wigwe seeks here to mould events in accordance with comprehensible human ambitions; what he has overlooked is the plan of the gods, which threatens and finally destroys human designs.

(3) How successful do you think Amadi is in persuading the reader to accept the intervention of the supernatural in the lives of the characters in *The Concubine*?

One difficulty which readers of *The Concubine* commonly experience is connected with the place of the supernatural in the novel. Ours is a fundamentally scientific age; consciously or unconsciously, we bring to literary works attitudes which might be called rationalist or materialist. It may thus be difficult for us to accept the credibility of a novel in which a supernatural world of gods exerts a crucial influence on the narrative. Had Amadi rested content to write about a simple village tragedy stemming from natural causes—the fight with Madume, Emenike's 'lock-chest', Ekwueme's dissatisfaction with Ahurole, and so on—such a gap in belief would not have arisen. But for him to do so would have been false to the ancient world evoked in *The Concubine*, a world in which thought and action are dominated by belief in the supernatural. In the plot Amadi is careful to supply a plausible causal explanation of events; but he overlays and supersedes this by an alternative version which traces the happenings to Ihuoma's origins in the spirit world and consequent fatal effect in human society. The narrator's problem is to give this second version convincing plausibility, and we should examine his methods in seeking to achieve this aim.

A writer dealing with supernatural matters has two alternatives: he can either treat them as exotic and alien to the world he is describing (as Shakespeare does, for instance, in *Macbeth*); or as an integrated part of his imaginative world, as Amadi does here. Whereas Shakespeare draws attention to the weirdness of the witches in the language and imagery of the play, Amadi is at pains to treat natural and supernatural as part of one continuous whole—in Omokachi, intercourse with the world of gods is an everyday matter which calls no special attention to itself. Man's relation with the mystery of the universe has been routinised. *The Concubine* convinces us because of its thoroughly-executed realism: human and supernatural events are described with the same evenness of tone and keen eye for detail. The reader is imperceptibly drawn into a world whose characters perceive no gap between real and spirit worlds, and through the intimacy and sureness of tone and cumulative realism of the detail, comes to endorse and believe in that world while he is reading a book. A good example of Amadi's art, drawing on folk-tale and oral tradition in which the supernatural is a pronounced feature, is Madume's consultation with the dibia in Chapter 11. A bald recital of the events recounted sounds improbable: attempting to make overtures to Ihuoma, Madume injures his foot; when he consults the dibia he learns that the injury is caused not by the buried hoe against which he has stubbed his toe, but by spirits from the sea who are punishing him for his advances. The little scene offers in fact a model of the entire novel: a seemingly natural sequence is ultimately viewed in a supernatural light. But this reading of events is couched in the most realistic terms; the catalogue of items for the sacrifices—alligator pepper, manillas, an old basket, cowries, unripe palm fruit, cobs of maize, plantains, fish, two cocks (one white), eggs, camwood, chalk, tortoise and chameleon—is so precise, so tied to the environment of Omokachi that the scene gains total credibility; even more so when Madume grumbles about the expense of the affair. The agency of the gods and spirits in a scene like this is not in some other world above and beyond, it is part and parcel of the routine of life. Trivial events gain significance from supernatural interpretation. Many other such scenes could be cited—Ahurole's hesitant visit to Anyika in quest of the love-potion, for instance—which attain the same degree of persuasive realism. Furthermore the agents of the spirit world in Omokachi—Anyika, Nwokekoro and Agwoturumbe—are invested with a variety of character which renders them human and relates them to their society.

Amadi's second strategy in making the supernatural convincing for the reader is his handling of group psychology. *The Concubine* is a fine analysis of a communal society in which co-operative endeavour, unity and solidarity of kinship are at a premium. Amadi shows this in countless instances—the aid given to Ihuoma over the second burial, the repairs to her roof, the tying up of her yams, the dance scenes, the marriage negotiations, the search and debate over the deranged Ekwueme, for instance.

Through the rhythms of this communal life founded in the natural world of the forest the reader gains an image of an utterly believable society. If the communal spirit expresses itself visibly in dance, farming, and debate, it also operates on an unseen level in the system of belief about man, the spirits and the ancestors. The people not only assume the reality of the gods, they guide their daily life by them. Even those like Madume or Ekwueme, whose actions shatter the repose of Omokachi by somehow challenging the settled order, are just as deeply affected by the gods as their more orthodox fellow men. This is fundamentally a community of belief with no dissident voice; the attitude is fatalistic—whatever happens is part of the gods' decrees. If we feel that the Sea-King, Amadioha, Ojukwu and the rest do not exist in 'reality', they exist most potently in the hearts and minds of Omokachi. From this firm and intense communion of belief the supernatural takes its reality.

It has been memorably said that literature dealing with the supernatural requires of the reader a 'willing suspension of disbelief'. When we enter the world of *The Concubine* we do need to abandon our modern faith in scientific rationalism—only another form of superstitition, after all. Through the realism of detail, the quiet undemonstrative tone, and the convincing dramatisation of tragedy in a community dominated by belief in the supernatural, Amadi creates in *The Concubine* a wholly convincing fictional entity.

Part 5

Suggestions for further reading

The text

The Concubine, Heinemann Educational (African Writers Series no. 25), 1966, reprinted 1977. The page references in the text of these Notes is to the latter edition.

Other works by Amadi

Novels:

The Great Ponds, Heinemann Educational (African Writers Series no. 44), London, 1969, reprinted 1975.

Sunset in Biafra, Heinemann Educational (African Writers Series no. 140), London, 1973, reprinted 1978.

The Slave, Heinemann Educational (African Writers Series no. 210), London, 1978.

Plays:

Peppersoup and The Road to Ibadan, Onibonoje Publishers, Ibadan, 1972.

Isiburu, Heinemann Educational (Secondary Readers Series), London, 1973.

Cultural and historical background

J.D. FAGE: *A History of West Africa*, Cambridge University Press, Cambridge, 1969, reprinted 1972.

ELIZABETH ISICHEI: *The Igbo People and the Europeans*, Faber, London, 1973.

———: *A History of the Igbo People*, Macmillan, London, 1976.

VICTOR UCHENDU: *The Igbos of South-Eastern Nigeria*, Holt, Rinehart & Winston, New York, 1965.

Commentaries on *The Concubine*

ELDRED JONES: in *Journal of Commonwealth Literature*, no. 3 (July 1967), pp.127–31 (review).

EUSTACE PALMER: in *African Literature Today*, No. 1 (1968), pp.56–8 (review).

———: *An Introduction to the African Novel*, (Chapter 4), Heinemann Educational, London, 1972, reprinted 1974. A straightforward brief account.

O.R. DATHORNE: *African Literature in the Twentieth Century*, (Chapter 3), Heinemann Educational, London, 1976. A brief, unsympathetic account of the novel.

ERNEST EMENYONU: *The Rise of the Igbo Novel*, Oxford University Press, Ibadan, 1978. Provides interesting background on Igbo literature.

EMMANUEL OBIECHINA: *Culture, tradition and society in the West African Novel*, Cambridge University Press, Cambridge, 1975. For the advanced student: detailed and expert appraisal of the West African social context, with many detailed references to *The Concubine*.

FLORA NWAPA: *Efuru*, Heinemann Educational, (African Writers Series no. 26) London, 1966, reprinted 1975. Another Igbo novel dealing with the same situation as *The Concubine*.

The author of these notes

ROGER EBBATSON was formerly Senior Lecturer in English at the University of Sokoto in Northern Nigeria. He was educated at Barton Grammar School, Lincolnshire, and at the Universities of Sheffield and London. He has lectured at Bromley College of Technology, Goldsmiths College, and elsewhere. The author of many articles ranging from slave trade literature to evolution in English fiction, he has published a full-length study entitled *Lawrence and the Nature Tradition*, Harvester Presss, 1980.